SECOND STAR TO THE RIGHT

BAILEY BLACK

Bailey's Other Books

Fantasy Novels

<u>The Lost Darling</u>

<u>Second Star to the Right</u>

<u>The Island of the Lost</u>

<u>The Cerise</u>

<u>Lucky in Love</u>

ROMANCE NOVELS UNDER THE NAME BAILEY B

<u>Broken Love Series</u>

<u>1. Beautifully Broken</u>

<u>1.5 Paper Hearts</u>

<u>2. I Hate You, I Love You Part 1</u>

<u>3. I Love You, I Hate You Part 2</u>

<u>Stand Alones:</u>

<u>Unexpected</u>

<u>Falling for You</u>

<u>In Too Deep</u>

A GIFT ♡ FOR YOU

Thank you so much for purchasing the paperback of Second Star to the Right!

If you're like me, you probably like to read in the dark, which can be difficult if you don't have a light or you have a partner who is a grumpfish and doesn't like the light. I get around this problem with ebooks and as a thank you for your support, I'd like to offer you a FREE ebook download on my website.

Head over to my website www.baileyblackbooks.com, or scan the QR code and find the Ebook titled **Wednesday and Naverland Book 2**. This is the discreet ebook version of this novel.

Use the code **Pan** at checkout and your ebook will be emailed to you through bookfunnel.

Download Your Ebook

CHAPTER 1
Peter

Wednesday's body hangs lifeless in my trembling arms, her head lax, falling backward, her limbs limp. The last words she whispered before passing out were, *"Help me,"* and it takes every ounce of willpower I have not to let my shadow take over.

I feel him under my skin, slithering like a snake, begging to be set free. My body physically cages him in and he riots against the binding, his magic pushing against my bones.

If I knew how, I would release him into the world again. Sharing our body is dreadfully unpleasant. In the realm of the living, we don't have a choice. My soul is forced to return to his former self.

A simple shadow.

A mirrored version of myself with no ability to move on his own and no voice to be heard.

I'm not a fan of silence. I like hearing my other half, especially when his thoughts are baleful.

"Let me hurt them," he shouts and I'm surprised to hear him again. *"I'll kill everyone that touched our Darling."* Shadow's rage tangling with my own creates a dangerous cocktail.

I want to rip the throat out of the person who hurt our Wednesday Darling. I want them to suffer. I want their heart to beg for release. I want to feel each beat until it finally stops, and then I want Shadow's magic to bring them back to life just so I can do it all again.

I want to avenge our Darling, but killing everyone on this side of the Island to find the sorry bastard isn't in the cards.

Not yet.

Shadow's impatience sends a burst of energy from my chest. The shockwave ripples through the air with enough force to blow napkins off the table and rock a wind chime.

I search the room, my eyes taking in every detail with a speed and clarity I don't usually possess.

Shadow's power rolls beneath my skin like a wave in the ocean. I can touch it and manipulate it, but he wields its true potential. He's connected to the Island in ways I can only dream of. It bends to his will and feeds off of his emotions. Even now, the clouds outside of the bar darken in the sky. Thunder rolls above us and I can feel the shift in the room's air, just like I would if I were to stand outside.

Lighting cracks somewhere overhead. A flash of yellow flickers in the gradually darkening bar. The room is empty, except for the drunk passed out in the corner and the shaky barmaid. At first glance, nothing looks amiss, but it doesn't take me long to notice four glasses on the countertop.

Two filled nearly to the top.

Two empty.

Sitting side by side in pairs.

Shadow's voice screams in my ears to burn down the bar and torture the maid until she squeals like a pig. I'm inclined to listen, but the featherlight woman in my arms keeps me somewhat grounded.

Still... someone did this to my Darling, again, and when we find out who it is, they will pay.

"I see you've met my date," my brother's voice croons from the doorway.

My shadow lurches at James with the intent to smother his lungs with darknes. Dark mist drifts toward my brother like a cloud of fog in the night, but it only stretches an arm's length away.

Shadow is tethered to me and his anger is a seething heat that over-powers my senses. I feel his desire to tear James to shreds and, while I am not my brother's biggest fan, he is still my brother.

My flesh and blood.

More than the bonds that tie me to the Lost.

The only living family I have left.

James's boots carry a heavy thud as he crosses the room. Our bartender visibly relaxes in his presence and I try not to laugh. Now that Shadow and I are bonded, I think I could strike James down with a bolt of lightning, should I choose.

And that's where the problem lies.

Most days, I don't want him to suffer.

My brother may have chosen to side with the Fae, but he doesn't hold their powers. He's still human, with an unbeating heart and a soul that can be saved. The day he sacrifices that, it's game over. I will have lost him.

"Your date?" I echo.

Shadow thrashes like a ship trapped in a glass bottle during a hurricane. Gusts of wind rattle the windows. Wooden shutters slam against the siding, and innocent people holler at each other outside on the street to find safety.

Shadow doesn't like the thought of Wednesday being in the same room as James, let alone his date. I don't either.

James's brows pull together and he frowns. He drinks in my Darling with his eyes, thirstily lapping every inch of her lifeless body. "What did you do to her?"

Wednesday shudders and gasps for air. Her lungs wheeze, struggling against whatever coils around her bones like a snake. I shift her in my arms and steady her head against my shoulder. I hear her heart rhythmically beating in her chest, but with each second that passes it weakens. Her life force disappears, like the sands in an hourglass, reminding me that time is precious and being wasted.

Still, I hold my composure. Appearances are everything. If James knows what the Darling means to me, to all of us, he'll tell his Fae bride. Wednesday will never have a chance at life if Belle knows she exists.

"I was about to ask you the same question."

"Don't be coy with me, brother," he snaps. "I just got here."

"Right, and I'm supposed to believe that's not your drink over there."

"It's not," James growls, his tone final. So much like our father.

A violent shudder rips through Wednesday. I hold her tighter, unable to breathe as I wait for the convulsions to pass. Seconds turn into a painful minute, and her seizure shows no signs of stopping.

Shadow grows weary. His nervousness turns my stomach. Another minute passes. Shadow's dark presence stops reaching for James and wraps around Wednesday like a blanket. He steadies her heart and slows her breathing. After what feels like a lifetime, her body calms, but she still doesn't wake.

"You're wasting time, Peter. Time she doesn't have!" Shadow yells at me.

He's right, but the adrenaline I felt when I walked into the bar is wearing off. I *need* Wednesday to be okay. Not because she's the key to breaking the curse or because she's Wendy's reincarnation. I need her to survive whatever this is because if she dies it will be my fault.

If I hadn't listened to Shadow, if I hadd just left her alone, she wouldn't be dying.

James grabs my elbow and tries to shift Wednesday out of my arms and into his. "I'll be taking it from here."

"Over my dead body." I jerk free of his grasp. Anger pours out of me in waves again; this time, it's just as much mine as it is the dark beast's. Shadow's darkness shoves James back a few steps, then wraps around Wednesday again. My brother's balance falters, but that small win does nothing to ease my fury.

"That can be arranged." James grins and the wickedness in his expression chills my bones.

I shoulder past and ignore his last comment. I don't want to fight my brother tonight. I can't guarantee Shadow will let him live this time, not when our Darling's life is on the line. But that doesn't mean I wouldn't put a dagger through his heart if it means Wednesday will live.

James follows me through the saloon's swinging doors and yells, "Peter!"

"Ignore him," Shadow urges, but I can't.

My brother sounds worried, an emotion I can say he never showed when Wendy's life hung in the balance. I turn to face him, unsure if the delay is a trap, but he genuinely looks concerned.

"Is she okay?" he asks.

I let out a heavy breath, two things coming to light at once. One, James knows Wednesday. The how is irrelevant; our Island is small, and I know she sometimes wandered. I let her because Shadow was always close enough to keep our Darling out of danger.

What concerns me, though, is how well they might know each other. How deep do my brother's feelings run for the other half of my soul? I close my eyes and swallow the sting of the past as it creeps up my throat.

The second thing I know at this moment is that James would hesitate if he had to kill her. What I don't know is for how long. How far will his defiance be tolerated before Belle forces his hand?

"I don't know," I admit. "But she will be."

I push off the ground, not wasting another minute, and shoot into the sky. I don't think about how James has never seen me fly or what the pirates will assume. My thoughts are on Wednesday.

Only Wednesday.

The sun begins its descent into slumber, twilight rising to prepare us for night. I know the direction I'm headed, like I know my shadow. To the second star, soaring until the magic of night ripples through the air and the sun crosses into the other realm. By sea or by sky, that's when the veil between our world and hers is thin enough to pass through.

It kills me that I have to do it this way, but I'm keeping my promise.

It's time to take my Darling home.

CHAPTER 2
Wednesday

I never considered how a single moment could change my life.

One decision, so seemingly insignificant at the time, has the power to affect everything.

As I lay here, unable to move, trapped in never-ending darkness, I try to pinpoint the moment my life veered off course. Most might say it was when I took a drink from a handsome stranger at a bar—who I think might have stalked me before that day—and then tried to kill me. But I could argue that my downward spiral began on January eighteenth.

That's the day I skipped my afternoon workout and came home early to find my twin sister and my then-boyfriend fucking on my brand-new couch. Who knows, maybe if I hadn't caught them, it would have been a one-time hookup and I would be blissfully unaware, cooking him a vegan dinner while he played video games on the leather sectional that I later dragged down to the alley from our third-floor apartment and set fire to.

Believe me when I say it was more therapeutic than the rebound dick I chased in the following weeks.

Or maybe I need to look further, all the way back to high school, to the first day of Biology when Kenny Dean Admire sat down next to me. There were still half a dozen open seats in the room, including one next to my sister, Tyle, but Kenny chose to sit with me. It was the first time I was put before my sister, and I was ecstatic.

Thinking back to that day, I can still feel those nervous butterflies springing to life. The excitement every time we locked eyes. The lust from something as simple as our fingers brushing against each other. It was magical.

If only I had the foresight to lie and say that I had a lab partner or maybe even agree to work together so long as we kept all of our interactions flirt-free, I wouldn't be in the situation I'm in.

Oddly enough, though, if I ignore the fact that I don't know where in Neverland I am, and that the two gorgeous men I trusted and gave myself to tried to kill me in their own wicked way, and that I've possibly been kidnapped twice in the last three weeks, I don't hate Neverland like I did when I first got here.

If given the choice, I'd do everything exactly the same because it brought me to Peter.

He's my fairytale come true.

The other half of my heart I never wanted until I knew what missing him would feel like.

He's a dick who has done everything wrong, but he's my dick, and as much as I want to fight the pull I feel to be with him, I can't. Wendy Darling, my past self, loved Peter. She was his soulmate, which makes him mine, too.

How?

I don't know. Logic rarely plays a part when the heart is involved and for me, that rings true. I can hate Peter. I can be so angry with him that I want to wring his neck, but when it comes down to the bare bones of how I feel there's no denying that a big part of me loves him, even though I wish I wouldn't.

A faint beeping carries into my thoughts. At first, I didn't notice it, but the sound continues until it becomes something I can't ignore. It echoes melodically in the dark, then beeps again. Louder this time. Again and again. And then there's a whoosh.

Beep. Beep. Whoosh.

Beep. Beep. Whoosh.

There's a tingle somewhere in the darkness, and I vaguely remember that I have arms. It seems silly, but I've been floating for what feels like forever with nothing but my thoughts to anchor me in the sea of night. My body is abstract, disconnected from my mind. Or maybe it's the other way around. I'm not sure. Just like I'm unsure if this is what unconsciousness feels like in the land of the living.

Dying and bright white lights seem to be synonymous with where I come from, but no one asks about the unconscious or the people in comas.

I wonder if this is what it's like for them? A never-ending night that stretches on like the sea, surrounded by nothing but memories and thoughts of what could have been until the world comes back into focus? If so, why does no one talk about it? Why don't we acknowledge the place between life and death? I have no doubt that's where I am.

In between.

The sensation in my arms grows stronger. It's pinprick-like but not uncomfortable, and then, without warning, I feel heavy. My whole body tingles and it aches from immobility. I try to move some part of me, any part, but nothing happens. I'm conscious enough to know I can move but not enough to make it happen.

If I could sigh, I would, but even my lungs don't follow orders yet. I remember this from the last time I was drugged. Waiting for my body and my mind to connect is torture, but at least this go around I know what to expect as I wake.

Except for that sound.

Beep. Beep. Whoosh.

I don't know what that is.

A cold breath of air pushes through my nose. It doesn't fill my lungs, but I'm not struggling to breathe, either. It's an odd feeling. One that makes me want to take in more air, and so I try, but my next breath is a mix of natural warmth and damp coolness.

It reminds me of the forever frost that coats the inside surfaces of all the cups in the Treehouse web. The thin layer of ice defies all logic, but I've seen it with my own eyes, and I've touched it with my two hands, so I know it exists. Just like I know without a shadow of a doubt that Neverland is real, Fairies—or Fae as they like to be called— can't be trusted, and magic is all around us.

Another cold breath pushes into my lungs and strangely enough, it makes me think of Cass. I was with him when I first felt the touch of Neverland's magic and it is because of him that I'm stuck in the between.

A twisted thought chills my bones. One I never considered before, but when you're trapped in your mind there's nothing to do but think, and this one thought has me on edge the longer it sits.

The air in Neverland was only ever comfortable near the tree-houses. There the cups were coated with forever frost, making our drinks cool and refreshing. When I drank with James, everything was at room temperature. Not uncomfortably warm, but not cold either.

Except for the drink I shared with Cass.

I only took a few sips, but now as I think back to it, my glass was chilled.

What if Cass is behind the frost? I know nothing about him, not really. Not the things that count.

Ugh, I have so many unanswered questions!

If Peter Pan is real and his shadow is a living entity separate from his body, why couldn't Jack Frost or some version of him be real, too?

Another question to add to my ever-growing list. I worry I'll be stuck like this and never get to ask Peter, but then that tingling sensation spreads to my toes and I remind myself I just have to wait.

CHAPTER 3
Peter

Days have passed.

Days of arguing with incompetent doctors.

Days of sitting in a painfully uncomfortable chair, watching machines breathe life into the other half of me.

The doctors don't do much. Shadow and I see them twice a day. Once in the morning. Once after the sun has set. They look at the numbers on the machines that beep and whoosh and tell us it'll be soon, but they never say when soon is.

I don't think they know.

The nurses are more helpful. They check on our Darling every few hours, making sure she's as comfortable as possible. Sometimes they turn her body to prevent something called bedsores. It's painful to watch as her limbs fall lifelessly in the direction gravity pulls. If not for the ability to hear her heart and the annoying beeps from machines that never cease, it would be easy to confuse her as one of the dead.

"This is taking too long," my shadow urges. He's restless. His magic hums under my skin like the tingle of a foot unexpectedly waking from sleep. I hadn't noticed the discomfort in Neverland, but here the pain worsens each day we wait for our Darling to wake.

"And what would you have me do?" I think to my shadow. He hears me as clearly as if I were to have spoken the words out loud. Just as I hear his grunt of frustration. He wants to use magic on her, but I'm worried about the effects it'll have in this world. Not just to our Darling, but to us too.

This realm is angry with our presence. She tolerated us when our visits were short, but as one day drags into the next, she takes from me. I'm tired. A kind of tiredness that rivals the pull of darkness and I'm afraid to close my eyes. I'm not certain this realm will let me open them again if I do.

"Find our Darling in the darkness. She's lost between the worlds and the longer she's there the harder it is to come back!"

I feel his fear. Neverland is a broken bridge between death and the afterlife. Most souls make it to their destination, but some—those with unusual trauma—get stuck all on their own. Others are stolen on their way to the afterlife. A problem my shadow has been battling for more lifetimes than we should be allowed to live.

But Wednesday is somewhere else.

A dark maze between the realm of the living and the dead. I only know it exists because it's where Shadow was created. I don't remember it, and I don't know how to navigate within its confines, which is why I'm hesitant to enter its clutches.

"We're wasting time!" he growls.

I don't disagree. Time may move faster in the realm of the living than it does in Neverland, but it feels slower. Back home, before the magic shifted, a day was measured by the clouds. Orange and pink hues meant our day had begun. When they shifted to bright blues and deep purples, we had passed into the evening. We had no hours to count. No minutes that crawled away. No second hand that ticked and ticked. The days came and went, but here—in this room that smells of chemicals and death—time is torturous.

"It's too dangerous," I caution. We would have to put my body to sleep somewhere and hope that I could find that realm. Hope I can locate her. Then pray that I can bring us both back. The plan relies too heavily on magic. Shadow may be willing to risk what little we have left on the endeavor, but I'd rather reserve our magic for a surefire save.

Shadow riots inside me. He pushes and fights to break free, but in this world, he's lucky to be more than a dark mirror forever stuck at my side.

He kicks and my leg jerks in response. *"You're scared because you're weak."*

I am.

Shadow's ability to control me, even for the slightest of moments, is proof. At this point, I don't know how to remedy my weakness. I feed my body the food this world provides and nourish it with the water they steal from the land, but it's never enough. No matter what I do, the pull to close my eyes and fall into the dark abyss is too strong. "Your point is moot."

"Let me heal you, Peter. Once you're strong, you can save her."

"At what cost?" Magic comes with a price and the cost of using it in this realm is steep. The day we brought Wednesday to Neverland a plane crashed. Most would find that tragedy purely coincidental, but the ten souls who lost their lives washed up in Neverland. They became prisoners of the Island and I think it is because of what Shadow and I did. "Whose life will be lost to extend ours?"

"I won't take to the point of death. You're not that weak yet, but you will be if we don't do something now!"

I pick at a straw wrapper and tear it into tiny pieces. "Save your magic for our Darling. She may need it more than me."

"I can't heal her if you're dead, Peter! I can't exist in this world without you. If you die, I die."

"I'm not dying," I whisper the words out loud but I don't believe them. One look in the mirror and I can see the toll this realm is taking on my body. It won't be long before I deteriorate into the dust I'm meant to be.

"Yet."

The machine that beeps in rhythm with our Darling's heart makes a new noise. A faster beep and then two slow ones. Then another faster one.

I don't get my hopes up. Twice now she's stirred and not woken, but Shadow is anxious. He fights my resolve to stay in the chair. I forfeit the battle, not willing to waste my energy on him, and stand by Wednesday's side. She groans and turns her head from one side of the pillow to the other.

Hope moves me to sit on the edge of her bed and grab her hand. It's a painful emotion. My stomach thrashes like a ship in the sea, and my heart races at the speed of a hummingbird's wings. I hate the sensation but cling to it all the same. "Darling? Can you hear me?"

Wednesday's eyes flutter open, but they're hollow. She stares up at the ceiling, her body awake, but her essence far, far away. She's soulless. A living beast touched by death. That hope I felt falls into a puddle on the floor. People aren't meant to return from Neverland. When they do, they come back broken.

"*Darling?*" Shadow says, his voice carrying out of my mouth. He refuses to accept that we gave Wednesday the same fate as Wendy. He takes her hand and sends a surge of magic from me to her.

My head spins the moment his magic leaves my body, but I feel it tug at something in the ether. It fights with forces I can't see, pulling at the woven fibers in my body. Whatever Shadow's magic wants feels like acid in my veins. I take a shallow breath, unable to close my eyes because Shadow is still watching Wednesday for signs of life. Still holding onto her with doleful desperation.

Wednesday sucks in a sharp breath. Her body shudders as it comes back to consciousness. She looks around and, this time, there's a warmth to her brown eyes. Her head tilts to the side and she finally sees me. The color drains from her already pale face, but then her lips lift into the most beautiful smile I've ever seen. "You're here."

I'm so relieved I almost laugh at the ridiculous thought that I would be anywhere beyond her bedside. I hated the minutes we were apart and made them as few as possible because I refuse to let Wednesday wake up alone this time, questioning her sanity and wondering where I am. No, I will stay here until she wakes or this realm claims me.

"Did you think I wouldn't be?"

Chapter 4
Wednesday

Bright white lights push their way through my eyelids. It's uncomfortable and yet I can't shy away from it, even as brown and yellow spots cloud my vision. With every beep and whoosh that permeates the darkness, the blotches over my eyes clear away. I recognize the sound somewhere deep in my mind, but the memory is blurry.

Beep. Beep. Whoosh.

My throat is dry to the point it burns when I try to swallow. I blink some more and white ceiling tiles take form. They're large, twelve-by-twelve squares, with specks of gray sprinkled throughout like stars in a hazy sky. The thought of being outside on an overcast day is comforting, but I'm nowhere near the outdoors. I'm in a small room that smells like bleach and latex, with too bright of lights and that incessant sound.

Beep. Beep. Whoosh.

Out of the corner of my eye, I see an IV stand. A clear bag hangs from it, tubes draped loosely, finding a home in the beeping monitor and then connecting to a venous catheter in my hand. It hits me that I'm in a hospital, and for a split second, I can't remember why that realization feels odd.

"Darling."

I turn my head to the sound of his voice, desperately hoping I didn't imagine it. Peter sits on the edge of my bed, cloaked in shadow. His hand holds mine and while I should be concerned that I can't feel his touch, I stare at him, shocked by what I see.

Peter looks nothing like the man I last saw in Neverland. Dark circles hang under bloodshot eyes. His cheeks are hollow, the skin clinging onto them in a way that reminds me of the dead. His dark hair is unkempt, oily, and possibly thinner. He's aged ten years in the time I've been here, and even though he looks days away from meeting the Grim Reaper himself, my heart races at the sight of him.

"You're here," I say, unsure of if the man I'm looking at is *my* Peter or something else.

He squeezes my hand and a faint tingle radiates from his touch. "Did you think I wouldn't be?"

Tears I can't control swell in my eyes. They fall down my cheeks in slow, steady streams. I can't explain the feelings I'm hit with. There are too many layers on top of each other, but crying feels good.

"Oh, Darling." Peter pulls me into his chest and holds me.

Weeks of frustration, grief, and fear pour out of me. My tears are silent but powerful, touching parts of my soul that needed a release from the weight it had been carrying in Neverland.

"I'm sorry," I whisper as I wipe my eyes. "I don't know where that came from."

"Never apologize for the feelings your beating heart carries." Peter touches my cheek. His hand is cold and calloused, more so than I remember. "Only the living can feel so fully. I'm jealous."

The blues of his eyes darken and black wisps of magic pouring into them. I know now what that darkness is. I remember everything from Neverland and even things from beyond, Wendy's memories. Gifts from when he pushed me off the Neverpeek mountain.

"Hello, Shadow," I whisper, cupping Peter's cheek. His lips twitch upwards and then pull down into a frown. The darkness I glimpsed fades away and I'm met with the same worrisome blues I've grown so fond of. "Are you okay?"

Peter takes my wrist and pulls my hand from his face. He looks at me with an intensity that makes me think he's searching my soul for lingering damage. "The question is, are you? I didn't think it was possible to fear for you more than I did in Neverland, but you've proven me wrong." He laughs, but the sound is forced.

I find the remote to my hospital bed and press the button to sit upright. The muscles of my back ache in protest. They've been still too long, angry from the time in this bed and likely the journey from Neverland home.

A shuddering thought crosses my mind. Peter killed me to bring me to his home. I don't want to know what he did to bring me back to mine.

"Tell me what's going on. Where are we?" I start with those questions because the one I'm dying to ask scares me. In nearly every story I've read the use of magic has consequences. I imagine Peter's magic does too, which could be why he looks like shit. I need to know if I've taken something from him or someone else in Neverland, but I don't think I can handle the answer if it is yes.

"We're at a hospital in Fort Lauderdale."

"Why here?"

"Because I was..." Peter's eye twitches. He grunts then corrects himself to say, "We were worried you wouldn't make it any further. Someone did a number on you again, Darling. Any chance you know who it was this time?"

"How is it possible both of you are in there?" I whisper, meaning to keep the question to myself but, like usual, I have a problem keeping my thoughts secret when Peter is involved. He draws my truths out of me without trying, and I unwillingly give them to him.

"It's not easy," Peter says, his voice huskier than usual. For a fraction of a second, the darkness clouds his irises again, but then that deep blue pushes through and Peter is solely himself again.

I watch him, waiting for a deeper explanation or answers to the questions he knows I'm thinking. *When did Shadow re-attach himself? How does his magic work in this world? What is it like to feel Shadow under his skin?*

Peter responds to my silent questions with a distant stare. He's here physically, but his mind is elsewhere.

I shift under the blanket and feel the stubble on my legs catch on the fibers. I pull them closer and run my hand across my shin. I fight a frown at the sensation. My legs aren't just stubbly, they've turned into a forest. I hate to think about what the rest of my body is like. I press my arms to my sides so that Peter can't see the hair that's probably in my pits and let my gaze sweep across the room.

My room is private, which is nice, not shared with a thin curtain to separate me and a stranger. The bed takes up most of the space, but I seem to be in a corner. My window is roughly five feet from me, in a narrowing passage, with a chair seated awkwardly between us. I have a bathroom to my right, presumably with a shower, and the door to my room is straight ahead. I can see the corner of the nurse's station and the rolling computers they take from room to room, but not the nurses themselves. All things considered, I'd say it's pretty private. A blessing since talk of Neverland would probably land me in the psych ward.

"Do you know where my clothes are?" I ask since that's one of the things I don't see. My shoes are nowhere in sight either. I'm hoping there's a closet in the bathroom that my stuff is stored in.

"Why?"

His question irritates me, but I try to keep my frustrations to myself. There's a lot Peter doesn't understand about this world, like money. As shitty as it is to say, he can stiff a bartender a few dollars on a drink. They'll be pissed, but no one will ruin his credit over it. Hospitals require names, birthdays, and Social Security numbers. Everything we can't honestly provide because red flags might go off about me. For all I know, my name is tagged as a missing person. As soon as someone realizes I'm awake, the cops could be called, and I don't know how to answer the questions of where I've been, who took me, or whatever else they might ask. "Because we need to get out of here."

"We're not going anywhere until the doctors are certain you're okay." Peter shifts in his seat. His leg spasms, kicking outward and striking the edge of my bed. Something is going on with him. The longer we're here, the more likely it is someone will notice, and that could be just as problematic.

"I'm fine. Honest." I wrap the blanket around my waist and scoot to the edge of the bed. Peter's at my side the instant my feet hit the linoleum tiles. My legs wobble beneath me, but I stay upright. There's a tugging sensation between my legs and I see a piss bag hanging off the side of the bed, connected to me by a catheter tube. I groan, embarrassed, and grab that along with my IV stand and head toward the bathroom. "But we need to get out of here. I doubt I have insurance anymore and I can't afford the bill attached to my stay."

"Everything is paid for," Peter insists. He wraps one arm around my waist and tries to usher me back into bed. "Sit down and stop worrying."

I don't sit. Instead, I poke my head through the bathroom door of my room. I was right about the shower being in there, but not about the closet. My clothes and shoes aren't anywhere to be seen.

My heart races with anxiety and the *beep beep beep* of the machines race with it. I need a shower and to put something on that doesn't expose my ass to the world, and right now neither is an option.

"How, Peter? Every day we're here costs tens of thousands of dollars. Do you have that kind of money?"

"Yes," he says flatly.

Peter curls his fingers over mine, and this time, I let him lead me back to the bed. He stands before me, and seeing how loose his clothes are on his body tugs at my heartstrings. He's wasting away and I don't know why. I wish he'd tell me what's going on, but like all the other questions I've ever asked my inquiry is ignored.

"I have an account overseas set up that anyone can access so long as they know the PIN."

"Sounds like a good way to get robbed," I mumble.

"Maybe, but I change the number every time I call for access. It's never the same number twice. If someone is smart enough to hack it, they deserve the spoils, but I promise there's more than enough in there for the both of us." He unhooks my piss bag from the IV stand and attaches it to the side of my bed. "Money isn't an object. Whatever you need, Darling, it's covered."

I need a lot of things, mostly in the form of answers, but I get the feeling that Peter isn't going to give those to me. He never does. He's skilled in the art of avoidance and redirection. In another life, he would have made a good lawyer. Or maybe a car salesman. "Can I ask you for a favor?"

"You could ask for my life and I'd give it to you, Darling."

There's a heaviness to his words that makes me think he's telling the truth. He looks so thin, so frail, I can't help but worry that's exactly what he's done.

"Can you run to the store and get me some clothes, and maybe a razor and some shampoo and soap? I want to leave this place as soon as possible, but I can't do that if I look and smell like an ape."

"I can if you promise to let the doctors look you over while I'm gone."

I'm positive the hospital staff has seen every inch of me more than once. I doubt another exam will make a difference, but if that's what it takes to get out of here, so be it. I call that an easy compromise.

"Okay, Peter. It's a deal."

CHAPTER 5

A young brunette pokes her head into the room within minutes of Peter stepping out of the room. Her big brown eyes widen when they settle on me. I give a small wave because what the hell else am I supposed to do?

"Oh!" the woman says quietly. She stares at me for less than a half-second, but it's enough to tell me that she didn't expect to meet my gaze. She doesn't wave back. Instead, she yells, "Doctor!"

The nurse hurries to my bedside and pushes buttons on the monitors that are tethered to me by stickers, a finger clamp, and a cuff. Squiggly lines appear on a small screen, then shift into new frozen lines. She pushes another button that brings the machine to life again and then it makes more beeping noises.

A few moments later, a man in a long white coat enters the room. His dark hair is slicked back, and his face is clean-shaven, but it's worn with little wrinkles. The tells of long nights with too little sleep and too much coffee. He sits beside my legs, on the bed, with a kind smile on his face that says *I'm your friend, Wednesday. Trust me.*

I'm not sure I can trust anyone in this world, let alone this hospital, but I smile back and hope it tells a convincing tale. *I am nobody worth worrying over. I am fine. Let me go on with my boring, completely normal life, and you'll never see me or my deteriorating friend again.*

I don't think the doctor believes my face. He picks up the chart hanging on the edge of my footboard and then flips through the pages. I doubt he's reading the words. My chart is an inch thick and he's done with it in less than a minute.

"Hello, dear. My name is Dr. Hall," he says, handing my file to the nurse. They exchange a silent conversation, using only a few glances, before he turns to me again. "Can you tell me your name?"

"Wednesday." My voice cracks and there couldn't have been a worse time for it to happen. My doctor lifts an eyebrow, losing faith in my *I'm fine* act.

The nurse hands me a small cup of water. I smile appreciatively and take a sip. The cold liquid is a shock at first. Ice clanks in the cup and I have to remind myself that the cups here aren't lined with forever frost.

I'm hit with an unexpected sadness that I'm no longer in Neverland. That place never felt like home, but now that I've left it, there's an ache in my chest to return. It takes a few seconds for me to get my bearings, but when I do, I try to convince Dr. Hall that I'm okay again.

"Roberts. My name is Wednesday Roberts."

He nods to the nurse and she scribbles something in my manila chart. I've always hated that about doctors. They write or type things about you, and you never see what is written. For all I know, the woman is playing a game of hangman and Dr. Hall's just signaled her a letter using their secret code. I could be billed for a fucking game of hangman and I would be none the wiser.

The nurse's badge holder twists on the lanyard around her neck. I can see her identification card and her name. Carmen Right. A pretty, used-to-be brunette who has on more makeup than Target carries. She's a walking TikTok filter. She is beautiful, but I have a hard time trusting a woman who feels she needs to hide herself behind a pound of makeup. Does that make me a judgmental bitch? Probably, but if I'm going to risk spilling any of my secrets, I need to know who it is that I'm talking to. I've seen some crazy videos where people look one way when they wake up and transform into a totally different person after an hour in the bathroom.

"Can you tell me what day it is?" Dr. Hall asks, and I'm embarrassed when I can't. I shake my head, so he prompts," What about the month?" When I don't answer, he tries, "Year?"

I let out a shaky breath. Tears of frustration prick my eyes because I don't know.

I don't know how long I was in Neverland or how long I've been lying in this bed. I don't know if my sister went through with the wedding or if our parents were so torn up about my disappearance that it was postponed. I don't know if my goldfish, Rocko, is still swimming happily or if he died from a dirty tank and neglect.

I.

Don't.

Know.

Anything.

I almost wish my lack of knowledge is from memory loss because that would be expected, but it's not. It's because my favorite fairytale came to life.

Unlike Wendy, who willingly flew into the night sky, I was forcefully taken. In a span of weeks, Neverland sucked my life away like it was a black hole. It made me forget things that were a part of everyday existence. At one point, I even forgot I wanted to leave because that's what Neverland does.

It makes you forget.

But I remember everything that happened there and I can't talk about any of it.

"Short-term memory issues are normal, Mrs. Roberts," Dr. Hall assures me. He pats my leg, like I'm a little kid and the sensation is anything but reassuring. I feel patronized and a little uncomfortable.

"You have what's called anticholinergic toxic syndrome. Confusion is an expected side effect. A few more CCs of saline and you'll start to feel like yourself again." He squeezes my knee and my hackles stand on edge. I don't like him touching me, but I'm sure the act is meant to be comforting, so I let it go. He stands, nonchalantly adding, "You were lucky. The poison used to drug you isn't something we've seen at this hospital. We almost couldn't figure out what it was."

"What was it?"

Dr. Hall writes something in my chart, then nods to Nurse Carmen. She steps up on instinct, as if responding to a conversation I wasn't privy to.

"I'm just gonna check your blood pressure, sweetie." She takes my left arm and slides it into a blood pressure cuff. It hugs my skin, creating enough pressure to make me wince, then releases with a beep. I understand the cuff's purpose, but I've always hated them. They remind me of being bound, unable to move. Something I've never personally experienced, but I've read enough books for my thoughts to stray to the dark corners of my mind. I don't think it's something I'd like.

My numbers appear on the small screen and Dr. Hall smirks approvingly. He scribbles what is probably unreadable nonsense on the papers in my file, then hands the nurse my chart again.

"We're gonna keep you another night or two for observation," he says as if I didn't ask him a question a few minutes ago. He clicks his pen and then tucks it into his jacket pocket. "I'm sure everything will be fine, but I want to be safe."

"If it's all the same, I'd like to be discharged," I tell him, irritated at having been ignored, but I'm picking my battles. Another day here is another handful of hundred dollar bills in his pocket. Dr. Hall is probably looking at me and seeing neon green dollar signs.

Too bad for him, I'm broke.

Dr. Hall and Nurse Carmen exchange glances. I don't like the look on their faces. I have the nagging feeling that his wanting me to stay might go beyond earning a paycheck. They're hiding something, which is bullshit because whatever it is, it's about me. I have a right to know.

I stare at them, waiting patiently for that look to turn into words, but no one speaks up. It's a reminder of the harshness of this world I'd forgotten about.

The only person who will look out for me is me. As soon as they leave, I'm going to read through my chart and find out what they're hiding because I get the feeling they won't tell me.

After a brief moment, Dr. Hall flashes a toothy grin and says, "How about we run some labs? As soon as those numbers come back, I'll sign the release."

"I don't want—" I don't bother finishing.

Dr. Hall leaves the room before I can ask him anything else, and I'm drawn back to a moment when I was a kid. Even for routine appointments, the doctors came and went in less than five minutes. It didn't matter that I had to sit in the waiting room for what felt like ages. I felt like they believed their time was more important than mine, and that same feeling rings true now.

Nurses, on the other hand, are never rushed. They take their time.

They are the soldiers in the medical war, making sure each casualty is taken care of with utmost care. They are unappreciated heroes.

"He means well," Nurse Carmen says with an apologetic grin. She adjusts the tubes in my IV machine and fluffs my pillows. "He's just a little brash sometimes."

"Why are we running another round of labs if everything is fine?" I ask her, hoping she will give me a straight answer and not some medical jargon I'll have to decode once I have a phone again—another item to add to the ever-growing list of things I need.

"Your husband said you were at a nightclub when you started acting funny. He thought someone had spiked your drink."

My husband?

Did I miss something major while I was out cold?

I glance down at my left hand and a certain finger is bare. The relief I feel is instant. I used to dream about the day I got married, and an unspoken goal of that day was to remember it. If I'm going to financially and emotionally tie myself to someone, I'd like to think that person and I would have lots of good memories together, that day being the best of them all.

I can't say Tyle feels the same. She's made it known her only plans on her wedding day was to look pretty and get shitfaced. You'd think she'd want to cherish the moment. After all, she must have been desperately in love with Kenny to steal him away. But no.

The bite of jealousy still stings, not because I want Kenny back. I'd rather let Cass kill me a thousand times over, in new brutally painful ways, than get back with that man. What hurts is that Peter's unconventional family—minus one...there's always one—is more loyal to him than my own sister is to me.

My twin sister.

And that hurts worse than any death I might face.

My relief of not having a wedding that I've forgotten twists into something darker, dancing on the brink of disappointment. I don't know if my feelings are turning or if these are latent emotions tied to Wendy's memories.

Apparently, I'm her soul reincarnated. I thought Peter was crazy, but when he pushed me off of Neverpeek Mountain its magic opened my eyes to more truths than I was ready to accept.

That being one of them.

Ready or not, I know it's true. When I look at Peter, I feel her longing. It's cold and full of sorrow, but then my own desire to feel his touch ignites a fire in my veins that only grows when it finds Wendy's gasoline. It's confusing as hell, especially when she loved him so deeply and I teeter on the line between lust and hate.

A flash of a memory I know isn't mine sparks in my mind. Peter stands on the sidewalk beside a brick building and an iron gate. He smiles at me—Wendy—and my heart soars. He tucks unmarked hands into the pockets of tweed pants and stares at me. I walk closer, taking in the subtle muscles outlined beneath cream-colored sleeves. His shirt is buttoned nearly to the neck, but it's open enough to reveal skin as pristine as a new canvas. He leans closer to say something, but I can't hear his voice. Whatever it is, my cheeks flush with delight.

I blink and the memory disappears. I'm back in the too-bright room that smells like bleach, lying on an uncomfortable bed in nothing but a paper-thin gown, staring at a woman I'm not sure I can trust.

"He doesn't wear a ring," Nurse Carmen adds as she tops my water cup with ice. "But he's shot down every girl who's hit on him with a cheesy line about you meaning more to him than life itself." She looks at me with adoration, then sighs. "He must really love you."

Peter's definition of love is borderline obsession. He shows kindness in his own ways and knows how to satisfy me physically, but he has no boundaries.

Obviously.

Most relationships don't start with potential stalking and kidnapping. Despite it all, Nurse Carmen is right. Peter does love me in the only twisted way he knows how.

"You didn't answer my question." I change the topic. Love isn't something I'm ready to commit myself to. Peter and I have a lot to learn about each other first and I'm going to need a ton of groveling after everything he's put me through before I even begin to consider opening myself up to those feelings.

Nurse Carmen glances at the open door to my room. She can feel Peter's presence even though she doesn't realize what the feeling means. He emits a dark tingle that creeps up your spine, exciting fear and lust all at once. It's because of the magic flowing through Peter's veins that we can feel him as he draws nearer.

Nurse Carmen visibly tenses. I'm sure she's worried about answering my question and assumes this sensation is fear of getting in trouble, but I feel it, too.

I reach out and touch her hand. She's so much warmer than The Lost. Their skin has a chill I'd grown so used to, I've forgotten it isn't normal.

Nurse Carmen sits on the edge of my bed and looks at me with worried eyes. "The doctors don't want to say anything because it's too soon to tell, but there may be side effects from the poison. Your labs are reading fine and the last two ultra—"

"Leave," Peter orders. The chill from his presence settles into my skin, his deep growl raising the tiny hairs on my arms. The way he stares at Nurse Carmen makes me shiver, and I'm not even the recipient of his fury.

She opens her mouth to argue until Peter's darkness cloaks the room. The veil is thin, unnoticeable to anyone who doesn't know what they're looking for, but there's a new heaviness in the air that squeezes my chest. I struggle to breathe even with machines pumping air through my nose. I can't imagine what it must feel like for my nurse.

She looks at me briefly, an unspoken apology in her eyes. Her fingers hastily wrap around the metal clip that attaches my chart to my bed. She takes the papers that detail what the doctors put me through, hugs them to her chest, and then leaves.

As soon as she's gone, Shadow's magic recedes. The weight in the room lifts, and I can take an easy breath again.

I push myself out of bed, not caring that my ass is exposed or that I look like I've been through three rounds with a broken hairbrush and lost.

I'm pissed.

That nurse was about to tell me what Dr. Hall wouldn't and Peter and Shadow's high and mighty attitude ruined everything. Now I've got to find a way to steal my chart or convince someone else to let me in the loop because I doubt that woman will come back in here ever again.

Peter tosses three plastic bags on the bed, hopefully with some clothes and toiletries.

I set my hands on my hips, ready to light into him, but once he turns his gaze to me I lose the ability to think. Dark matter fills his irises, only leaving the thinnest ring of deep sea blue at the edges. It lingers, devouring more and more of the royal blue in his eyes until there isn't any left.

"Shadow?"

Chapter 6
Wednesday

The Shadow I met in Neverland was of the playful kind, with an air of mystery to him. His magic seemed to have an extra layer of depth that sometimes made me shiver, but I was never afraid of its abysm.

He'd walk through the woods, sometimes as if he were a part of it, and the Island's shadows would reach out to touch his darkness. The animals came to him as if he was their friend while the Lost disregarded him as nothing more than Peter's silent other half.

To me, Shadow was someone I could talk to no matter the subject. He knew the secrets I refused to tell Peter, listened to my questions and answered as many as a silent man could. My body may have belonged to the King of Neverland, but my mind and heart were Shadow's.

I can easily say he was my best friend in Neverland, but there's something different about him here. A primal instinct deep in my mind urges me to run far away even though my body won't listen. My heart races in my chest, wildly throwing my senses out of whack. I could cry and puke all at once from nervousness if only my body would give in to its urges.

"I prefer Pan," he drawls. Unlike Peter, who sounds American with a slight hint of something else, Shadow has strong undertones of the same mysterious *ish* James's voice carries. An alluring accent as sweet as the Devil's candy. Addicting and potentially lethal. "But I do like the way Shadow sounds rolling off those pretty lips."

Fear wraps itself around me like a noose. I can't control the tears that pool in my eyes or the way my body trembles. I can't make my voice steady or my heart stop racing. I can barely keep myself from cowering, but I manage to stand upright and pretend to be brave when I ask, "What happened to Peter?"

Pan—the only reason I'm not calling him Shadow is because this version of my friend makes the name feel dirty—ambles around the room, looking at everything as if it's the first time. Perhaps it is. He doesn't try to hide his disgust at what he sees. It's written on his face in the way his lips turn down and his brows bunch together.

"Peter and I don't belong in this world, Darling. The longer we're here, the more your realm will try to reclaim us." He drops into the oversized chair in the corner of the room, sitting sideways so that his legs hang over one armrest and his back reclines against the other. He threads his fingers together behind his head, acting as if my world trying to kill him is table talk at tea time. "Your precious Peter would have let us turn to dust in this death castle if it meant staying by your side until you woke."

"Doesn't sound like you feel the same." My legs threaten not to support me any longer. I lean against the plastic footboard of my bed, shielding my exposed backside from him and the nurses in the hallway. I don't know what Pan means by *turn to dust*, but the way Peter's body was withering away I'm thinking sarcasm and metaphors for something less cryptic might be out the door.

"I reap death, Darling, not succumb to it."

A new wave of goosebumps roll over my skin. I believe, without a shadow of a doubt, that Pan has killed things in Neverland. Possibly people, too. If he has—and I'd be willing to bet the answer is yes—there's a good chance he might have been the catalyst that brought The Lost to Neverland.

Hell, he could have been the reason I was taken there, too.

The thought is dizzying. I grip the edge of the footboard and try to act like the nagging thought that Pan might have targeted me doesn't bring me to my knees.

If there was a prize for the unluckiest woman, I'm pretty sure I'd be the winner. My ex-boyfriend is a cheater. My rebound a kidnapper. My fuck buddy a murderous backstabber. And now this...

My best friend is a manipulator with stalker tendencies.

Watching Pan control Peter like a puppeteer pulling strings on his marionette, existing as one person and not two bound together, sparks the idea that everything that has happened to me could be Pan's fault doesn't seem as far-fetched as it should.

My chest aches and the *beep beep beeping* of my heart monitor lets everyone within earshot know that I'm freaking out. I hope I'm wrong.

"Death castle?" I ask, my mind reeling.

A new thought, that Shadow could have used Peter's body to kill me, crosses my mind. That would make him my kidnapper, not Peter. Heat climbs my neck to my ears. I clench my teeth and try not to lose my shit. Shadow made me feel like I could trust him. He tricked me!

"Seems fitting," he says casually. "Castles employ people to do their bidding. Cooking. Cleaning. Execution." He flicks his wrist, gesturing to the hospital and the walls that confine us. "This facility has multiple people to aid in the deaths of those it ensnares. It's genius for its generation. No one suspects what's going on."

"The doctors don't kill people here!" I snap. The venom in my tone has nothing to do with defending the staff. My shock turns into anger, and I'm so mad at Pan that I could cry. "They save them."

"Are you sure about that, Darling? I could feast on the souls on this floor alone and the people you call doctors would bring me more without even blinking." Pan stares at me, those dark irises daring me to ask the next question.

I'm not sure of anything, Pan. Thanks for asking. "I'm gonna take a shower."

Pan's jaw tics. I think he's mad I didn't lead us down the rabbit hole of questions like he wanted, and that has me biting back a grin. I hope the feeling festers under his skin and brings Peter back to the fore-front. I can't stand to look into Pan's dark eyes and question every interaction we've had over the past few weeks.

"Make it quick. We need to leave within the hour."

I laugh, baffled at how out of touch he is with reality. I want to leave this place just as badly, but the reality of what I want and his unrealistic timeline is that we're going to be here for a while.

"Nothing in a hospital happens in less than an hour. There's paper-work that needs to be filled out and bills that need to be paid, and that's only for discharge. If Dr. Hall gets the labs he wants, we have to wait for the phlebotomist to come to the room, draw my blood, and then take it down to the lab, where we wait for the results to be put into the computer. At some point before the end of Dr. Hall's twelve-hour shift, he'll look at them and tell us what's going on. And then we might begin the discharge process."

Pan grunts, his gaze laser-focusing on my face. He stands effortlessly, where I would struggle to get out of the awkward position, and grabs the bags he purchased. He shoves them to my chest and glowers. "I will happily kill everyone in this building if that's what it takes, but I promise you, we will be outside of this death castle before the sun dips beneath the horizon. Mark my words."

"You wouldn't."

"I would." Pan leans closer. His breath caresses my cheek as he whispers, "I'm nothing like your precious Peter, Darling. He is the clouds in the sky and the water in the sea. I'm the darkness brought on by the storm and the monster hiding beneath the surface."

The balloon in my chest deflates. I feel like I'm falling, tumbling down the side of an emotional mountain. Sure, I'm angry, but that heat is taking a backseat to the hurt I feel.

I thought Shadow was my friend.

I thought he cared about me.

"Why are you being such a jerk?"

Pan grunts and drops back into the oversized chair. "Go take your shower, Darling. The clock's ticking."

I bite my lip to keep it from trembling and grab the bags he brought me. I look straight ahead, refusing to make eye contact or look down. Any shift and the tears will fall. I don't want him to see me cry.

I slide the bathroom door closed and lean against it. My mind tries to process that I'm home and that Peter is gone, but it circles back to how heartless Pan is and drowns in the hurt.

My throat burns when I try to swallow. I'm losing the fight with myself to stay ahead of these feelings. I'm about to reach for the shower curtain when Pan's deep voice carries through the paper-thin walls.

It's a gruff whisper, but I hear him clearly when he says, "Because you'll never love me, Darling. The best I can hope for is hate."

CHAPTER 7
Wednesday

I liked the web of treehouses Peter and the Lost lived in.

The tiny, one and two-bedroom wooden houses are high off the ground, keeping us from predators and, amazingly, from bugs. Their kitchens are small, without modern amenities like a refrigerator or microwave, but their bathrooms have the usual toilet, shower, and sink.

I never asked where their running water came from or where the black and gray water went when discarded. I chalked all of that, and the lack of saturation on the ground, up to the magic of Neverland, and let it be.

But hot water, warm enough to soothe the tired muscles of the body and turn my skin red without causing a burn, doesn't exist there.

Neverland's showers are summertime pool warm.

Comfortable, but not satisfying.

This is a level of heaven the living take for granted.

I don't know how long I've been under the shower's spray. I let the water pressure beat down on me until the air is thick with steam. When my chest aches with each inhale and I'm coughing more than breathing, I shut the water off.

I didn't grab a towel before stepping into the shower because there's a stack of them on the rack above the toilet, which is only an arm's length away. The whole bathroom, sink included, is maybe six feet from wall to wall. It's small by the standards of what I used to live in but comparable to the treehouse bathrooms—an unexpected comfort.

I cover my face with my hands and give myself another second to process. I'm having a hard time wrapping my brain around the fact that Peter brought me home. I'm nowhere close to my family or the city he took me from, but I'm back in the real world and less than a day's drive from being in my bed again.

I'm eager to see my parents, which feels silly to be excited about. Before Neverland, I'd go months without seeing them and sometimes weeks without calling. I let the day-to-day grind of life steal the five minutes it takes to pick up the phone. Maybe it's because I knew I could always call or could go see them. I didn't mind letting the days slip by because there was always tomorrow.

In Neverland, I had no way to tell my family I was okay. There was no electricity or cell service. I couldn't even write a letter because there wasn't a postal service to deliver it. My family was left wondering what happened to me for days, maybe even weeks.

I could call them now, but I think the shock might be too much. Besides, I don't want to just hear my mom's voice. I want to hold her because I know both of us are going to be blubbering messes. Hell, my sister may have even grown a heart throughout all of this. I'm not holding my breath, but I'm not gonna lie; I'd be pretty happy if she cried too.

I pull the shower curtain back and metal rings slide across the rod. I cringe at the sound. It echoes in the small space and makes my ears hurt. Neverland's showers were exposed. Nothing separated the falling water from the toilet or the sink. It was an open area without division, and don't ask me how, but there was never water all over the floor.

"Towel?" Peter—I mean Pan—asks.

I know the man before me isn't Peter because his eyes lack the blue I've grown used to seeing, but my heart and Wendy's emotions struggle with the differentiation. The pull to give in to him is as strong as ever, maybe even more so now that I know we are soulmates. I ache to feel his hands run down the curves of my body, even though my mind protests the desire. But Pan isn't the man I've unwillingly given my heart to.

He's something else.

Something I'm not sure I can trust.

Pan leans against the edge of the sink, long legs stretched out, almost touching the side of the shower-tub-combo. Thick tattooed fingers hold my terrycloth. The semi-translucent ink is new. Peter's sleeve of twisting artwork stopped at his wrists, but Pan has the sketch of a realistic eye on his left hand and symbols over his knuckles surrounded by wisps of smoke.

Pan doesn't shy away from looking at my naked body. His eyes roll over my curves, slowly tasting me with each shift of his gaze.

I cover my tits and lady bits the best I can with my hands. He may look like the other half of my soul, but he is not Peter. He has not earned the privilege to see my body, though I can't help feeling aroused by the way he's looking at me.

"What the hell, Pan?" The new name feels weird on my tongue. If he hadn't turned Shadow into something provocative, I'd still call him that to his face.

I should save that name for when he's inside me.

No! Stop it, Wednesday. You are not allowed to fuck the crazy shadow man. This is where I draw the line. Two psycho kinda-not-boyfriends are enough.

Pan holds the towel out, a devilish grin on his face, waiting for me to take the terrycloth. I swear, if he can hear my thoughts, I'm going to strangle him.

"Relax, Darling. It's not like I haven't seen you naked before."

I groan and snatch the towel from his hand. I wrap it around myself, not bothering to dry off, and then cross my arms. "So, you've been spying on me."

He laughs, but it sounds nothing like Peter's light-hearted vibrato. The deep chuckle burns a hole in my heart. It's a reminder that Pan is a separate person and that Peter might be somewhere trapped in his mind. "Look around, Darling. What do you see?"

A psycho.

A creep I don't trust.

A murderous stalker who played the part of my friend to manipulate my emotions, hoping I'd never discover the truth.

"I don't know. A bathroom."

"Exactly. You only see what's staring you in the face, but everything in this room casts a shadow. It's there whether you notice it or not."

He motions for me to look at the small spaces. I hate to admit it, but he's right. The sink, toilet, shower rack, hell, even the toilet paper on the roll has a shadow. I guess I've always known where there was light a shadow existed, but I never equated any of that to him.

"Except for you." I twist the water from my hair, pretending to be uninterested in what Pan says, then let it fall over my shoulders again. Truthfully, it scares me that he has no shadow in this world. I don't know what it means for Peter or our future. If we even have one.

Do I want one?

I can't think about that yet. Peter and I can't begin to figure out what we are if one—or both of us—get hauled off by the police. "I thought you said we were in a hurry."

"We are."

I lift my eyebrows, silently hinting for him to give me privacy. It's clear he won't leave on his own, so I erase all possibilities of anything happening between us. Knowing Peter, that's what he would be waiting for. I can't imagine Pan's motives would be different. "Then get out so I can get dressed!"

Pan stands but doesn't leave. He comes closer, popping the bubble that is my personal space, and steps into the shower. I take a step back and realize there's nowhere to go. My bare shoulders press against the shower wall, and my damp towel clings to my skin. I cringe. The thought of the germs that might be on the tiles gross me out, but what other option do I have?

Pan grabs my wrists and pins them above my head. I struggle against his hold until my arms decide they don't belong to me anymore. I want them to pull and fight, I want my legs to kick him in the nuts, and I want to thrash like a wild animal until Pan gives me back my personal space, but all I can do is stand there and glare.

The worst part, he knows it.

Pan leans closer until his cheek touches mine. A surge of lust races through me. I close my eyes and fight the need I feel. I subconsciously lean into Peter's body, wishing with all my might that he would come back to me.

Pan's breath tickles my ear when he whispers. "I've only ever seen you through Peter's eyes. Touched you through the sensations met by his skin. I will take all the time I want, Darling, because you are a beauty that needs to be appreciated. I can feel your hesitation and taste your fear, but you're just as much mine as you are his."

I swallow the lump in my throat. There's a tingle deep in my stomach. I don't want to want Shadow. He's not Peter, and yet there's a new slickness between my legs.

Pan drops my arms and steps back, out of the shower. The air between us lightens and a weight on my chest lifts. "You have ten minutes to get dressed before I walk out those doors."

"What happens if I'm not ready?" I call after him.

Pan stops in the doorway. He grips both sides of the frame, his back muscles flexing beneath his shirt. "Then I'll pick your ass up and carry you." He looks over his shoulder, that wicked grin in place. I hate how my heart flutters and how my skin aches to touch him. Most of all, I hate that Pan knows how much I crave him. He knows I can't control my physical reaction to his body and I think he likes it. "Best put your clothes on quickly, Darling. I'd hate to kill anyone who looks at what's mine."

CHAPTER 8
Wednesday

I don't know how he did it, but Pan has my discharge release in hand by the time I finish getting dressed and blow-drying my hair. I put my clothes on as soon as the bathroom door closes, but then take my time to style my hair. A hair brush can only do so much when sea salt and wind factor into your daily routine. Ponytails and braids became my go-to style, but here all I have to worry about is humidity. I don't have tools like a curling iron or a straightener, but a lot can be done with a round brush and blow dryer.

I look in the mirror, pleased with my appearance, then open the door. Pan stands outside, glowering, but he doesn't toss me over his shoulder or carry me out of the hospital like a brute. He grabs my things and hastily shoves them in a leather duffle back and he *does* carry down the hallway.

"Excuse me," the hospital's security guard says as we near the exit on the ground floor.

I hold my breath, bracing myself for Pan's backlash. We've made it this far without confrontation and paid the bill without throwing chairs. Walked past a dozen doctors and nurses without so much as a death threat. We were so close...

Pan turns and smiles at the man. "How can I help you?"

"You dropped this." The man sheepishly holds a pair of black underwear that must have fallen out of my bag.

I blush and snatch the undergarments, embarrassed. "Thanks."

"Good looking out." Pan salutes the guard with two fingers. The man nods in acceptance and we continue out the doors. I side-eye him every step of the way, unable to figure out where the personality change is coming from. How did he go from a murderous psycho to a cordial member of society?

As soon as we're outside, Pan snatches the panties from my hands and tosses them into a nearby trash can. "You won't be wearing anything another man has touched."

There he is. I roll my eyes. "Possessive much?"

"Yes," he states flatly.

I cross my arms and keep my mouth shut the whole walk to the parking garage. It's only across the street, but it's long enough to get my point across that I'm not happy. In the bedroom being dominant is a turn-on, but I'm not for someone telling me what I can and can't do beyond my sex life.

I watch Pan as we cross the street, scrutinizing everything from the way he walks to how his jaw clenches every time he looks at me.

There's something different about him. Physically, he looks better. His cheeks are fuller, his skin less pasty, and he's filling out his clothes again. But the change runs deeper than what Pan looks like. The air of mystery that surrounded him when we met down in the Keys is coming back. I want him to look at me and talk to me, and not because I like the guy. There's a string wrapped around something inside me that makes my chest physically hurt if I don't have his attention.

The feeling reeks of Shadow's magic. Thanks to the Neverpeek, I recognize the sensation is more than hormonal desire. I also know that the change comes with consequences. Pan is sacrificing *something* for Peter to get better.

I try not to think about what the price for Peter's health might be as we climb three flights of steps. Someone—Peter or Pan, not sure who—parked their car on the top floor of the building. My legs cry out with each step. They haven't worked this hard in a long time. Lactic acid pools in my muscles. They burn and ache, and even though I'm in pain, I can't make my mind stop replaying Cass's last words. *Peter's magic is tied to his life.*

The more he uses it the quicker it kills him. Pan is not high on my list of people right now, but if healing Peter means killing himself, I have to stop him. One life isn't more valuable than the other.

"How are you doing it?" I ask when we reach the rooftop of the parking garage. There's one car parked in the center of the floor.

That's it. And a singular camera hangs outside the stairwell door, but it's old and unlikely to have audio. I don't worry about anyone hearing our conversation.

"I need you to be more specific, Darling. I've done a lot of things in the last twenty-four hours." Pan pulls a ring of keys from his pocket and twirls them around his finger.

"How are you healing him? And why isn't he back yet if you are?"

Pan stops walking and presses a button on his key fob. Headlights from the silver sports car flash.

"Peter is resting," he says after a pregnant pause. "His body grows stronger, but he is weak. Whether he knows it or not, he needs this recharge because the moment we cross into Neverland, I'll be kicked out of this body and he won't get another chance to heal."

I reach for Pan's arm. It's the first time I've touched him since I woke up. My stomach jumps, and my nervousness makes me giddy. His skin is warmer than I expected. Peter's hands were as cold as ice though the rest of his body was a touch warmer. Here he almost feels life-like.

Pan looks down at my hand, surprise dancing in his eyes. I touch his cheek, feeling the familiar tug of emotions I'm not ready to accept. I need time to process Wendy's emotions and determine where I stand. Peter is not Pan. Both men betrayed me but both men hurt me. And even though they are separate people, I worry about them both the same.

"What is healing Peter doing to you?"

"Nothing," he says far too quickly.

I chew on my lip and gauge how much knowledge I'm willing to share. Peter liked to dance around the truth like he was afraid of what might happen once I knew things. Pan seems to be the opposite. I think he wants me to understand his world and my place in it.

I hesitate for a heartbeat, then decide to see if he can validate some of what Cass told me.

"I know the magic is tied to your life and using it is risky. Probably even more so in this world. I want Peter to get better, but not if it means losing you in the process. You are my friend, Shadow. Despite everything you've done, I need you to be okay too." As soon as the words leave my lips, I realize I mean them. I don't want Pan to hurt, even if I am pissed at him.

Pan swallows hard. For a split second, I think I've broken through his jerkface facade and found my friend again but the softness I saw in his eyes vanishes. Pan's features harden again and the air around us drops ten degrees.

"You don't know the first thing about magic." He turns away and walks toward the headlights that flashed. "The sun will be setting soon. We need to get going."

"Then teach me!"

Pan ignores my plea and pops the trunk of a sports car open. He drops my bag in the back and slams it shut.

"Where'd the car come from?" I ask. I don't know what it is. I'm not a car person. Besides knowing that it's silver, two-door, has the Corvette logo, and costs more than I used to make in a year, I'm clueless as to what it is.

"Peter bought it." Pan walks around the passenger side and tosses the keys at me. "For you. Hope you can drive a stick."

"Nope."

I toss the keys back and Pan catches them with one hand. I don't want the car. It's too flashy, and if Peter had mentioned anything to me in the ten seconds I got to see him, I would have said as much. "Guess you'll have to take it back."

"Not likely." The headlights flash again when he unlocks the car. He walks to the driver's side and slides into the seat. He starts the car and pushes a button to put the top down. It latches into a secret compartment behind the seats, disappearing as if it never existed.

I don't know why, but I'm nervous. Maybe it has everything to do with the stream of thoughts warning me to be wary of Pan, or maybe it has something to do with the fact that I have no idea where he plans to take me. He's not bound to the promise Peter made to bring me home. He's not bound to anything beyond existing within Peter's body.

Pan turns the radio lower and looks at me with arched brows. "Any day now, Darling."

"No." My voice is a whisper lost in the night, but he hears it.

I think he chuckles darkly, but it's hard to tell over the sound of the engine. Pan unclicks his seat belt and gets out of the car.

"I'm torn, Darling," he says, walking around the front of the vehicle. "I'd hoped you would make this easy and follow directions, but I'm glad you're not."

The fingers on my right hand twitch. I look down at the spasming muscles and try to take control again, but Pan's magic wraps around them like a thin glove. My arm bends at the elbow. I watch my hand flex without command and my wrist twists to show the back of my hand first, and then my palm.

"You like that. Don't you? Controlling me."

This time, I hear the sound that vibrates in Pan's chest. "You have no idea what I'd like to do with you, but it's no fun if it's not consensual."

My cheeks heat. He wants to fuck me. I can work with that. Everything that happens to my body is my choice. I chose to manipulate Cass, even if it was done poorly. I chose to sleep with Peter. Now, I'm choosing to use my body to get answers.

I lean against Pan's side and press my chest into his arm. Not the smoothest of moves, but it'll get the job done. "I'll happily get in if you tell me where we're going."

Pan's brows bunch together. "I thought that was obvious. I'm taking you to your family."

"Oh." Maybe he is tied to Peter's promise after all.

"But first." Pan slides his hand to the back of my neck. His fingers lace through my roots, gripping and pulling my face upwards. I look into those eyes, curious to see if there is a trace of blue, but all I see is my reflection in the darkness. "You and I are going out to eat."

"Why?"

"Because you want answers and I may never get the chance to be with you again. It's your choice how far we take our relationship, Darling." He drops a singular kiss to the nape of my neck.

I suck in an audible breath. Pan's lips are a drug sweeter than anything this world offers. A taste isn't enough. All they do is tease my body and make me want more. "I promise to let you know my limits; if you promise to tell me everything Peter wouldn't."

Pan steps out of my personal space and opens the passenger door for me. "You won't like what you hear."

"You don't know that." I slip into the seat. It's lower than I expected and I almost fall into it, but Pan is ready to help me get situated with a steadying hand.

"I do, Darling." He closes my door and looks down at the ground as he rounds the car again. I can't hear what he says next, but I can read his lips when he adds, "I really do."

CHAPTER 9
Wednesday

I stare out the window as Pan drives us through town. The engine purrs angrily when traffic halts us to a stop. His foot is lead, wanting to race down alleyways and around cars, but the traffic lights every ten feet stop us every time.

I think Neverland altered my brain chemistry because I find it odd how so many people can co-exist without interacting. Strangers walk past each other, ignoring the presence of the person next to them. They talk on their phones and drive in their cars, and not one person bothers to smile at anyone else.

In Neverland, the Lost are always a part of each other's lives. As for the pirates... well, I don't know how close they are, but they would nod and smile at everyone they walked past. I miss that feeling of familiarity. Even in the cove, where I only knew James, I felt safe. I could roam freely without fear of being harmed because I was friends with him and the pirates were his allies.

In my realm, everyone is your enemy. No one trusts their fellow man, especially the ones who are suffering, and I find that heartbreaking.

Pan pulls the car up to a valet stand at a side entrance of the mall. I didn't know malls offered valet services. The one we have in my hometown is half-dead with more empty stores than people who shop. I'm guessing this mall is busier with a richer clientele than the one I'm used to.

"Good morning, Miss," a young kid says as he opens my door. He holds a hand out to assist me out of Pan's tiny death trap, then trades a claim ticket for the keys.

"Don't talk to her," Pan growls. He wraps his hand around my waist and ushers me into the mall.

Once we're inside, I step out of his hold and stop near the entryway. I cross my arms and shift my weight to one hand. "We need to talk."

"Is that so?" Pan shifts to face me.

"You've got to stop being such a jerk." I drop my arms and point behind us. "That man was just doing his job."

"I highly doubt his job included flirting with you."

"He was being nice!"

"He was trying to take what is mine!" Pan booms.

A few passersby stop walking to look at us, but no one says anything about the outburst. They look at us, eyes wide, probably judging Pan for yelling and me for allowing the conversation to happen. It makes me anxious to know that people are looking at us even as the shoppers keep walking.

"I don't belong to you," I whisper, my voice holding all the strength I can muster. "I am a person, not a possession. Either you start treating me like someone you care about and not something you own, or I'm done. Done with you. Done with Peter. Done with Neverland."

The words feel like acid in my mouth. My heart breaks and falls to pieces at my feet. I haven't had time to sort through my feelings and decide what I want from Peter. A friend. A lover. Something more that spans the galaxies and defies time. Cutting the cord on whatever we are feels like selling myself short of something that could be amazing, but I refuse to be in a toxic relationship.

Pan's eyes soften. He sighs, his shoulders rolling forward slightly. "I'm sorry."

"You're not forgiven, but I accept the apology." It's more than Peter ever gave me for all his wrongdoings.

Pan's lips lift slightly. The armor around him falls for a moment and I think I see the shadow I befriended on the Island again. He holds out his hand. "Walk with me?"

I take it and this moment feels like a glitch in time. This is what new couples did when I was in the ninth grade. They'd stroll through the mall on a Friday night holding hands and killing time for the sake of it. Back then, no one my age had a job or money. The guy I liked used to save his lunch money to take me to a movie and I would get twenty dollars from my parents to buy us dinner.

I have no clue what day of the week it is, and Pan supposedly has more money than I'll ever know what to do with, but this feeling—holding hands and window shopping—is nostalgic. It makes me giddy.

"Let's go into this one." Pan reaches for the handle of one of the shop doors. The big-name stores have roll-up doors that are open all day, but a few of the more expensive shops have glass doors. This is one of those stores. The kind of place I would never step foot in because a shirt is probably a hundred dollars and I can't even afford a sock.

"Are you sure?" I hesitate. Pan holds the door open for me, patiently waiting for my mini panic attack to subside. He said not to worry about money, but I do. I have none, and throwing away God knows how much on an outfit stresses me out. "I don't need anything this fancy. I'm sure Malley's or Sunningdales will have a nice dress I can wear for dinner."

"They might, but I already rented out the store."

My jaw drops. He did not. Tell me he did not! I look around and sure enough, there isn't anyone inside. Only two ladies stand behind the counter, practiced smiles in place, waiting for us to come in.

"Shadow," I whisper because I don't know what else to say. The gesture is painfully sweet and a little bit creepy.

"I don't want to hear another word." He sets his hand on the small of my back and escorts me inside. "Let me spoil you. It's the least I can do."

"Hello, Mr. Darling," The brunette with bright red lips says when we step inside. "I have the rack you requested ready in the dressing area. Mindy will serve your refreshments and we will both be here should you or your wife need assistance."

"Thank you," he says flatly. "But we'll be just fine."

I follow him to the back of the store where the fitting rooms are. The rooms are set up like a bridal shop, with each section having its own viewing area and a mini stage.

We walk to the furthest dressing bay and Pan gestures to a rack of dresses. Gowns both long and short, sequined and feathered, hang in order of color. I run my fingers over the hangers and stop at a green one that catches my eye. I check the tag and almost choke on air when I see how expensive it is.

"I can't." I look up at him with pleading eyes. "These are too expensive."

"Darling." He takes my cheeks in his hands and dips his head until our foreheads meet.

Time slows when we touch. Nothing matters except the way he makes me feel. I'm spiraling out of control, but have never felt safer in my life. This man will be both my savior and my undoing.

"I'd buy you the world if it meant more time with you." His husky voice vibrates my center. The way I'm feeling, it's hard not to believe in instant love. I wonder if this is how he feels, torn between what is logical and what is *us*. "Don't deny me the satisfaction of seeing you happy."

Damn this man and his ability to make me remember what living feels like. Life was easier when I existed in the moments between lust and hate. "I'll make you a deal," I finally say. "For each dress I try on, you've got to answer a question."

"Done," he says without hesitation.

I finger through the hangers and pull out a couple of dresses that catch my eye. "Real answers. None of those twisted half-truths Peter likes to give when I ask questions."

"I wouldn't dare." He takes the dresses from me. "Let me help."

I allow it because I think a part of Pan is hardwired to be chivalrous. He and Peter grew up in a different time, when in an age where men opened doors and women were cherished. He sets the dresses on the hanging hooks for me.

"Thank you."

"I'll be right out here." He tips an invisible hat and walks back into the viewing area.

I close the door and start stripping. I step out of my jeans and grab the first dress off the hanger. It's a flowy, red thing with feathers falling from the waist in cascading lengths down to my heels. It's hideous, but every dress is an answer given. I'll try on the whole damn store if that's what it takes.

I hold it and my girls with one arm and reach for the door. "Can you help me with the zipper?"

Pan stands. His eyes run over my curves as he comes near. He smirks, liking what he sees. There is no mirror in the dressing room.

I'm forced to step onto the small stage to see myself. I face the wall of glass but don't look at myself. My gaze is fixed on Pan, watching his expression as his hands roll up my back.

I bite my lip and fight another rush of desire. My body craves him like it craves chocolate during red-week. All I get are tastes, snack-size fixes from his touch that aren't nearly enough to satiate me.

Pan's fingers trail down my arms once the dress is secure. Static bounces between our bodies, torturing me. He's close and yet too far away at the same time.

"Anything you want to ask me, Darling?"

Right. Questions. That's the whole reason I agreed to try on this stupid dress. I clear my throat and turn to face him. "What are you?"

"Starting with the heavy stuff." He chuckles lightly, but the way he stands, the stiffness in his arm as he runs a hand through his hair, tells me he's on edge. "One day, I just existed. I could feel the Island. I could communicate with it, just like I could communicate with Peter." He shrugs and tucks his hands into his pockets. "Been here ever since. Next dress?"

I nod and he undoes the zipper. I hold the fabric to my chest and return to the fitting room. I close the door and let the gown fall to my feet. My back presses against the cold surface of the wall. It tethers me to this room and this moment. I squeeze my eyes shut and wrestle to keep my emotions in check, but it's a losing battle.

I'm struggling with sorrow. I can't imagine how hard it must be not to remember where you came from or who your parents are. What it must have been like to be alone when he came into existence. Tears pool in my eyes for him. They fall down my cheeks when I blink, carrying sympathetic sorrow. I wipe them away and grab the next dress.

"If I wanted to go back to Neverland, how would I do that?" I ask through the closed door.

"You want to come back?"

I walk out again, holding another dress to my chest. I didn't like this one on the rack and hate it even more now that I see myself in it.

Pan grins and shrugs. "Want me to zip that one?"

"No. The yellow washes me out." I turn on my heels and hastily go back to the fitting room. I don't know what's wrong with me. I've always had big emotions, but they're magnified today. I feel everything so much more intensely than I ever have. Even drunk me doesn't compare to this. *Did I come back broken?* " I don't know yet, but if I did, is it possible?"

"When the sun meets the horizon the path between our worlds is open."

"For how long?"

"That's another question. Do you have another dress on yet?"

I shimmy into a strapless shimmery number that squishes my girls and open the door. This dress is pretty, but it hugs too tight. My back will be hurting after a few hours. Plus, the way I bloat after eating, I'll look three months pregnant in this number. "Happy?"

"Depends on where in the world you are. As soon as day turns to night the portal closes." He looks over the off-the-shoulder dress. "I like this one. The green makes your eyes pop."

"That doesn't make sense. The sun was still in the sky when Peter pushed me off the boat."

"That's because you were in the Bermuda Triangle. It has wormholes strewn throughout it. Twilight, lightning storms, waterspouts, or any anomaly it deems fitting can open a passage into our world, but it's not consistent. Unless you possess Neverland magic, which Peter did, the living can't cross through. You have to die at the exact right moment to *possibly* find yourself in Neverland."

"Your magic makes no sense!" I say, frustrated. I change out of the strapless and slip on a deep blue number. The color reminds me of Peter's eyes. Dark with shimmery bits. As soon as it's on, I know it's the one.

I walk into the viewing area and Pan's face lights up. He looks at me as if it's the first time we've ever met, like our past and Peter and Wendy's never happened.

I meet his gaze in the mirror. "What do you think?

He pushes off the wall and stands behind me. One hand splays across my belly, pulling me into him. The other wraps around my neck. He tilts my face with his thumb. My heart hammers and my body hums, desperate for more of this man's touch.

That tug in my chest, the string that wrapped itself around my heart when Peter and I first met adds a new loop, tightening its hold. I have to remind myself that the man who holds me is not Peter. He's something else, but at this moment, my soul no longer feels as if it's been split in two. For the first time since Peter has come into my life, I feel whole again.

"You're the most beautiful star I've ever seen, Wednesday."

A smile tugs at my lips. I don't know why I expected something simple like *you look nice* to come out of his mouth. Nothing about my life has been simple since meeting this man.

Pan's head dips to the crook of my neck and presses the gentlest of kisses to my skin. I suck in a breath, surprised by how much it makes me wish his fingers would press tighter and pull my lips to his.

He doesn't hear my silent plea. I get that singular kiss, and then he steps away. Cold air fills the spaces where his body was and I find myself wishing I was in his arms again.

"Keep the dress on. We'll pay for it, then find some more suitable shoes."

I look down at my bare feet and wiggle my toes. "What's wrong with my Converse?"

Pan drops to one knee and picks up my sneaker. I slide my foot out, reverse Cinderella style, and he unties the laces for me. "These don't show the world how beautiful your legs are." He helps me out of my other shoe and ties them together by the laces. "But if your sneakers make you feel beautiful, then we will find a pair that matches better."

It's not that my shoes make me feel beautiful. I'm just comfortable in them. They're the security blanket in my life. Something I know won't let me down. I can run if I need to. I can walk without wobbling or falling. They make me feel like me. So far, they're the only thing since coming back that does.

"I have one more question... for now."

Pan frowns. "I have a feeling I'm not going to like this one."

"Why me? I know you said I'm Wendy's soul come back to life, but why now? Just... why?"

Pan sighs heavily and turns away from me. He ambles around the room, touching the dresses and fingering the jewelry. Doing anything but looking at me. "I've dreamed of you before I knew what dreaming was. Before I even knew what I was. My world was shades of gray seen through my own eyes but experienced by the hands of someone else. I spent years wrestling with the emotions Peter so freely gave up and learning what my place in the world was. I thought I'd found it as a guiding force keeping Neverland and its creatures safe from the Fae."

I sit on the armrest of one of the viewing chairs. I sense that out of everything I've asked, this is the hardest question to answer. "Is that what you do? Keep the Island safe?"

Pan nods, finally looking at me. "It was until you came into existence. Somewhere across the galaxies, your soul resurfaced. I felt it the moment you took your first breath, a painful longing pulling me away from my home. I searched for what felt like a lifetime before I finally found you. You were a child, maybe eight years old, when I first saw you through the window. You were playing with your sister, pretending to be princesses." He touches his chest, a far-off look on his face, and smiles. "Something inside me bloomed that day. I knew you were my other half, but you were so little. I knew from Peter's memories how important it was to let you grow up. So, I returned to Neverland but never for long. I came back every Neverland night knowing time would carry on in my absence. When you were finally old enough to make the trip with me, you'd fallen in love."

I shake my head. The only person I've ever loved was Kenny. I went on dates and had boyfriends, but none of them made me feel the way Kenny did. And he couldn't make me feel the way Peter and Pan do. "How is it possible to fall in love with someone if we're soul mates?"

"Love is a powerful magic in itself. It heals just as much as it hurts. Your heart can experience it as many times as your life allows, but your soul is only ever destined for one."

"What would have happened if Kenny and I had gotten married?"

A shadow falls over Pan's face. He shrugs. "I'm not sure. Lived a happy life, I guess, but I think a part of you would have always hoped for more. More attention. More compassion. Just... more. I left you alone because you were happy. I stayed as nothing more than a shadow in the distance, keeping a periodic eye on you, making sure you were okay."

"Until I wasn't."

He nods. "I think you can figure out the rest."

"Don't you think it's weird you've stalked me since I was a kid?"

"Only if you think it's weird that some part of you feels happier and more complete right now than you have all your life."

He's got me.

I wish it weren't true, but Pan is right.

He strides across the room and takes my hands in his. He looks down at me, pleading for forgiveness and understanding with his eyes. "I know our time is limited, just like I know you may never forgive me for what I've done, but I will do everything in my power to make it up to you."

Pan can never make it up to me. I'll never get back the days stolen or the time lost with my family. The best he can hope for is acceptance and for us to move past it. Sometimes, I think I'm ready to let go of all the hate and anger. Other times, I want to drown in it because it keeps me level-headed. "Who took me? You or Peter?"

"We both did. I couldn't have brought you over if it wasn't something he wanted, but it was my idea."

I nod, unsure of how to process that. Both men are guilty. Just like both of them stole different parts of my heart. I pull Pan in for a hug. I think we both need one right now.

He was right; I didn't like the answers he gave me.

The truth is never easy to hear, especially when it hurts, but I'm glad I got it.

CHAPTER 10
Wednesday

I don't feel good.

I don't know whether it's nerves or motion sickness from being in a car so low to the ground the past hour, but my stomach turns inside itself.

It hasn't been happy since Pan and I had pizza in the food court of the mall. I guess it could be the food, too. Everything we ate in Neverland was grown there. We didn't add chemical preservatives or red dye number *whatever* to enhance the taste.

I don't think a few weeks of whole foods can change the way my stomach processes food, but I guess it could be possible.

Pan pulls in front of the restaurant's valet stand. The lady running the car service ignores me and heads straight to him. I don't blame her. Pan is gorgeous. Somehow, his muscles are more defined here than they were in Neverland, and there are new tattoos on his body that were never on Peter's. The magic used to heal Peter is transforming their body into something that is purely Pan's.

Pan hands the valet woman his keys without so much as tossing a passing glance her way and rounds the front of the car. He opens my door and holds out his hand for me to grab. "Darling."

Sparks fly under my skin from where his hand holds mine. I feel guilty being attracted to him. Pan may look like Peter, but he's a different man. A beast made of magic, a shadow that fills the spaces inside me I didn't know were hollow until he touched them.

"I feel silly," I say sheepishly, looking down at myself.

We spent over two hours at the mall shopping for shoes and jewelry to go with the dress. Pan found me a pair of royal blue Converse and even though I insisted we keep searching for shoes that better matched the dress, he bought them. They sit in the trunk along with a pair of strappy stilettos I liked—but can't walk in—and a pair of *Disney* Princess pajamas he caught me looking at.

I thought we were done shopping after Pan picked out a white gold teardrop necklace and a pair of dangly earrings that matched, but we weren't. He took me to the spa—an actual freaking spa where they put you in a cotton robe and serve champagne— to have my hair styled and my makeup done. The ladies there plucked, rubbed, and did my makeup better than I could ever dream of, keeping my face subtle yet stylish. Everything felt amazing, but I don't look like me.

At least, not any version he's ever seen.

"You look beautiful." Pan is dressed equally as nice in a deep blue button-down shirt that matches my tea-length dress. It hugs his arms and chest, showing off enough dips and divots that anyone who dares to stare is teased by what could be underneath.

I know what Peter's body looked like underneath his clothes. Every curve was hard, but every edge was soft. His muscles were made by his way of life. Defined but not bulging. His ink carefully placed to accentuate his beauty. Looking at Pan, I can't help but wonder what new artwork might be hidden beneath that shirt.

My cheeks flush. I'm hot, even with an ocean breeze blowing from behind the building. Our reservations are at some five-star restaurant in the Horizon Hotel. I've never heard of either place, but *my date* swears they have the best Filet and lobster in the country.

Pan kisses my knuckles and then intertwines his fingers with mine. We walk through the hotel lobby and are quickly seated on a private terrace overlooking the water.

Within seconds of getting comfortable, our waitress appears. "Good evening, folks. My name is Molly and I'll be your server tonight. Can I start you off with something to drink?"

"Whiskey and coke," Pan drawls.

It's hard not to smile. I remember the day we met—well, Peter and I—and how he was doing his best to pretend I didn't exist while watching a football game. He sipped on a whiskey and ordered one again on the glass-bottom boat tour. It gives me hope that Peter is somewhere in there, fighting to get back to me. I miss him.

"And for you, Miss?"

"Just water, please."

The girl hurries away to get our drinks. Pan reads over the menu. He periodically mutters about what's offered, but I'm not paying attention. I stare at the vast span of darkness beyond the shoreline and listen to the waves crash along the sand. A knot forms in my chest. It sounds like home and it hits me how much I miss Neverland.

I miss the way the wind blows through the trees.

I miss the fireflies floating in jars. Their lights bright enough to guide my way but not overpower the stars in the sky.

I miss the smell of burning cedar and the tacky eighties music the Lost played through an ancient stereo.

I miss my friends.

Most of all, I miss being free, which is ridiculous because I felt trapped the whole time I was there.

But since coming back, nothing feels right, not even my own skin. It's too tight. Breathing hurts. Eating is uncomfortable. And my head has a light throb that won't go away. Emotionally, I'm up and down more than a yo-yo and I don't know whether I want to fuck Pan or stab him. It's exhausting.

Pan touches my cheek. I jerk out of my thoughts and look into his eyes. They're still dark, without any hints of blue, but there are wisps of charcoal gray in them that bleed into specks of gold and light brown.

He tucks a strand of hair meant to lie loose on my cheek behind my ear. "What's running through that pretty little mind of yours, Darling?"

I sigh and try to focus on the menu in front of me. The words are blurry. I close my eyes, take a deep breath, and then open them again. They focus on the letters, and even though I can read the menu, nothing looks appealing. "Nothing important."

"On the contrary, if it's bothering you so much as to worry your mind, I'd say it's rather important. Tell me."

"I just miss it. That's all."

"What?"

"Neverland." I peek up over the plastic-covered paper. A question hangs on the tip of Pan's tongue, but I'm in no mood to give answers. So, I ask one instead. "Do you know what you want to eat?"

Pan's lips lift into a delicious smirk. I can practically hear what he's thinking. My cheeks heat as I tell him. "I'm not on the menu."

His eyes light up, delighted that I know what he wants. I might want it, too, but for the time being, I'll keep that tidbit secret. "Perhaps for dessert, then."

"Can I get you anything else?" Molly asks as she collects our plates."Dessert, maybe?"

"I don't think your chef offers what I'm craving." Pan winks at me and that damn rush of heat floods my cheeks again.

"Try me," our waitress replies eagerly. "We're very accommodating."

Pan pulls his debit card from his wallet and holds it in the air. "Not interested, but thanks."

Molly takes his card to her kiosk and is back with the slip for him to sign minutes later. Pan tips her generously, then stands and pulls my chair out for me. It's hard not to like him when he's like this. Men aren't chivalrous anymore. Sure, women may get the occasional opened door, but all the other customs are gone.

"Do you want to go for a walk along the beach?" he asks.

"I wouldn't mind seeing the ocean." I let him lead me to the steps that descend to the beach. I hold onto the railing and look up at the sky. The moon is large, just shy of full and the stars twinkle brightly around it.

"You see that star?" he asks, pointing up at the blanket of darkness. "Second one to the right of the moon. Wendy used to call that the wishing star."

"Did you know her?" I stop on the second to last stair and find the wishing star in the sky. *Make a wish,* the little voice in my mind whispers, but I don't know what to ask for. I have too many needs. There's not enough magic in all of the worlds to grant me everything I want, and no wish is greater than the other. Instead, I settle on something temporary and easy to satisfy. *I wish to have no regrets about tonight.*

"No, not personally, but the few times Peter and I came together I could see her through his eyes." Pan taps his temple. "You'd be surprised at how detailed his memories are."

Silence fills the air between us. I like it so much better than the honking of horns on the road or the clamor of background music every building we've gone into. The sounds in Neverland were intentional, if anything at all. It was peaceful living in serene calmness until choosing to stimulate the mind. Standing out here, under the stars, listening to the tide roll in, I finally feel like I can relax a little.

"Are you ready for that walk?"

"Are you going to drown me again?" I side-eye him, half joking and completely serious at the same time.

Pan chuckles. He drapes his arm over my shoulder and descends down the final steps of the staircase. I go with him because I want to believe he is the same Shadow I knew on the Island. I want to trust that he won't hurt me.

"I was wondering how long it would take for you to figure out it was me who pushed you off the boat and not your precious Peter. He hated my plan. We argued for hours about how to bring you to Neverland."

"He once said he was trying to figure out what to do with me."

Pan stops to pick a shell out of the sand. He walks to the water's edge and rinses it off. "He was trying to convince me that we could bring you to Neverland alive."

"And you decided murder was the best route?"

Pan holds the bright red cockle up for me to see. He proudly slips his treasure into his pocket and begins searching through the sand again. "Are you ever going to let that go?"

I walk beside him, deciding to participate in the shell hunt. Looking for brightly colored or oddly shaped treasures is easier than looking at Pan. "Probably not, but if it makes you feel better, I'm not angry. I still don't trust you, but I'm glad you brought me there. It was a magical experience."

I bend down and pick up a piece of sea glass. The round edges are smooth, except for one corner where the ocean hadn't finished buffing away the harshness of its past life. It cuts my finger. I curse under my breath and stick it in my mouth.

Pan perks up immediately and drops the shell he was looking at. "Are you all right?"

"I'm fine." I pull my finger out of my mouth and show him the little wound. There is no blood seeping from the hole, even after my saliva dries from the skin. "See? Nothing to worry about."

But I am worried. I should be bleeding, even just a little. We keep walking, but I'm done picking up shells. The next time I look at my finger, the wound is gone. No cut. No scar. No sign that I was ever injured to begin with. The longer we walk, the more it bothers me.

What if I really did come back wrong?

What if I was never meant to return from Neverland and I'm some sort of living dead now?

My stomach twists at the thought, threatening to bring back the biscuits and chowder I ate. I bump into Pan's chest and look at him curiously. I must be losing my mind. He wasn't in front of me. He was to my side, off to the right, walking in the water.

Wasn't he?

"Don't lie to me this time, Darling." Pan tucks his thumb under my chin and drags my gaze to his face. "What's bothering you?"

"Am I like the Lost now?" My voice cracks. I'm about to cry again and I feel stupid for not being able to control myself. These tears are going to be the death of me.

Pan takes my hand and sets it over my chest. I feel my heart racing beneath my breasts. Each *thump thump* vibrates through me until I feel my pulse in my wrists and neck. He looks me in the eye as he says, "You are nothing like the Lost, or Cass, or even Peter and myself. You are living and breathing. You are growing. You've got a life inside you more precious than you'll ever realize."

"Take me back with you," I say suddenly. "I don't want to be here anymore. I just want to go home to Neverland."

Pan sighs heavily and pulls me into a hug. "I wish I could, Darling, but I can't. You need to be here because you can die. This is the safest place for you until I figure out who wants to hurt you."

I nuzzle into his chest. I don't want to be left behind. I want to stay in Pan's arms, which scares me more than living in either realm. "Does Peter agree?"

"It was his idea."

I yawn. I don't know why I'm so tired. I was fine a minute ago, but now all I want to do is close my eyes.

Pan lifts me into his arms. I curl into his body, pleased at how even though our stance has changed, we fit like cut glass. He carries us back toward the hotel and at some point, I fall asleep. I don't dream of Peter or the adventures I had in Neverland. I dream of Shadow, the dark creature in Peter's human form, and I'm not ashamed to admit I like the things he does to me.

CHAPTER 11
Wednesday

I jolt awake.

Bright light filters into the room. My heart races as I wait for my eyes to adjust. For a moment, I forget that I'm back on Earth and fear Cass has me. I'm not afraid of myself. I'm scared for Peter and the twisted plan Cass has for him.

My fingers grasp at the sheets beneath me. Within seconds, I can see my room, and the tension in my chest eases. I remember that I'm back in my world, heading to see my family, with a man who confuses me.

I push the crisp cotton sheets aside and step out of bed. My dress is still on, zipped up in the back, and my panties and strapless bra are in place. All I'm missing are my shoes, and even they are waiting for me on the floor of the bed.

"Pan?" I call out, walking toward the bathroom.

He pushes open the door dividing my room from the one adjacent. "I'm here, Darling." He leans against the door frame and tucks his hands into the pockets of his gray shorts. "Did you sleep well?"

My throat goes dry at the sight of him shirtless. He's stunning, more so than my dreams had imagined. The tattoos Peter had inked onto his skin are darker, filled with shaded details that are new to the art. Peter's pleasantly sculpted body now looks like it's been carved from marble, the soft edges hard and sharp corners deadly. I itch to run my fingers down those abs. I want to know if they're as firm as they look or if somehow our bodies are still molded to fit together. My sides are squishy, not hard, and my abs are hidden under a layer of love and pizza. Does a man with a body like that eat pizza?

"Um...what are you doing over there?"

"I figured you'd like some privacy. Can't win brownie points if you wake up with a man you don't remember going to bed with."

"Right." I look down at the ground. My ears are probably as red as a rose. I'm so embarrassed I fell asleep on the beach. "I'm sorry about last night. I don't know what happened to me."

"Love." Pan takes my hand in his and kisses the part of my palm that's beneath my thumb. The sensation shoots down my core and to my center, the feeling intoxicating. "You had a long day. I was selfish for not letting you rest sooner."

"I'm not a napping girl."

"Maybe not, but your body has gone through many changes since coming home. You need time to adjust." His lips slide down and press against my wrist. "To heal." He kisses up my arm. "To grow." Paving a path of lust until I'm breathless and his mouth is on my collarbone. "Sometimes your body just needs things you aren't ready for."

My body needs him.

It longs to feel his thick length inside me. It wants to know how Pan moves compared to Peter, and I feel so guilty pining for another man.

The Lost share lovers, but this isn't Neverland and Peter and I have never ventured down that road. What would he think if I slept with Pan?

Can this be called cheating if I'm not sampling a different dick, just a new driver?

"I'm," I say breathlessly. I close my eyes and fall into the feeling of bliss coming from his hands as they caress the sides of my arms. "I'm going to take a shower."

Pan's fingers find the zipper of my dress. He slides the little metal piece down my spine until it hits the stopper. I shiver, and he kisses the soft spot on my neck again. "No one is stopping you."

I turn to face him and look deep into his eyes. It would be easy to walk away. I could thank him and disappear into the shower, then use the water's spray to satisfy the need pooling inside me.

But I don't want to.

I slide one dress strap off my shoulder and then the other. The shiny blue fabric falls to my feet. Pan watches me, his eyes never leaving my face, even as I reach behind my back and unclasp my bra. "What if I want you to stop me?"

Pan doesn't hesitate. He wraps his hand around the back of my neck and pulls me into him. He kisses me like a man starved and I'm his last meal. Savoring. Devouring every ounce I give him.

I drag my nails down his spine. I want to hurt him so he can feel all the pain he's caused me, and then I want him saying my name the moment that pain shifts into pleasure.

I break the kiss, my chest heaving, and look into his dark eyes. All I see is lust. All I feel is desire. "Your move, Shadow."

Pan smirks, accepting my challenge. He grips my thighs and lifts me into the air. I wrap my legs around him. He drops us onto the bed and kisses me again, his hands moving with skilled desire to my lace panties. He rips the lace effortlessly and tosses it on the ground.

"I want to taste you." Pan presses my legs open. His tongue dives between my folds, licking and lapping, flicking and teasing my center.

I claw at the bedsheets, my back arching because I'm so painfully close to coming. My world spins and I'm not thinking about Peter or what Pan might be doing differently or better. I'm not thinking at all. I can't. All I can do is enjoy the ride.

Pan stops right as I'm on the edge and bites the inside of my thigh.

"Please," I beg. The build-up is so intense it's painful. I *need* some part of him inside me. Preferably his dick, but I'll settle for his fingers if that's all he'll let me have.

Pan presses fevered kisses on my leg. His fingers dig into my hips. His grip is bruising, but I want the pain. It teeters me that much closer to my release. "Please what, Darling?"

I grab Pan's hair and pull him to look at me. "Fuck me. I asked once. Now I'm telling you. Fuck me, Pan."

"As you wish." He pulls me to the edge of the bed and kisses me. I taste myself on his lips and my sweet musk makes me even wetter.

Pan drops his shorts and aligns himself with my center. He pushes inside with a deep, big thrust. I thread my fingers through the back of Pan's hair and take hold. I don't want his mouth leaving mine. I don't want to look into his eyes and feel guilty for loving this.

I just want to *feel*.

Pan eases in and out, giving me time to adjust. I moan, a sigh of pleasure releasing some of the tension inside me. He takes that as an admission that I'm ready and thrusts deeper, harder, finding a steady rhythm. It hurts a little, but I like it when he hurts me. I like how good the pain feels.

I let Pan control my body and mold me to his liking. He pushes deeper and I cry out, unable to keep the intensity of the pleasure to myself. His fingers curl around my neck and he pulls me upright, letting gravity control the pressure, and grabs my wrists. He presses them to my lower back and holds both wrists in one hand, making sure he's the only reason I'm upright.

"Say my name, Darling," his husky voice whispers.

I can't. I'm so close to coming. I'm scared that if I do anything besides enjoy the ride I'll miss the wave.

Pan adds a little more pressure to my neck and it sends me over the edge. A rush of pleasure ripples through me. I shake in his arms and cry out, "Shadow, god, Shadow!"

He arches me upright when I stop trembling and kisses me near my ear. "Good girl."

I'm catching my breath, my body already tingling with anticipation of more, when Pan pushes me downward. With my face pressed into the mattress, he thrusts harder, his balls slapping against me, and I'm coming again when his warmth spills inside. My body hums, happily accepting its penance.

Pan pulls out and kisses the space between the dimples on my back. "Thank you."

I slide onto my belly and rest my head on my arms. That was the hardest, best orgasm I've ever had, but it took a lot out of me. I'm tired again and might just take a nap after my shower. "For what?"

Pan chuckles lightly, then walks deeper into the room. He starts the shower, warms the water, and then comes to my side again. "Let's get you cleaned up."

I force my body upright and take the towel Pan has waiting for me. It's not a pretty sight, holding it between my legs as I walk to the bathroom, but it's better than all the little Pans dripping onto the floor and stepping on sticky cum covered carpet later.

I step into the shower and pull the curtain closed. Pan opens it a second later.

"What are you doing?"

He cups my cheeks, his lips finding mine, and steps in with me. He turns us so the water falls onto his broad shoulders and doesn't spray in my face while we kiss. I love the way our bodies feel together, how mine hums in delight, and his seems like it's made for me.

He smiles when he breaks the kiss and the sight is more beautiful than it should be. "Enjoying every minute I can get."

CHAPTER 12
Wednesday

I'm sore, but it's such an amazing feeling. I let the shower's water fall across my back and close my eyes. I can still feel Pan's hands on my skin. The way they caress my body, touching my tender places with utmost care. So much touching, and petting, and licking. My lips lift into a grin, my heart racing thinking about all the ways he's claimed my body this morning.

The only reason I'm alone in the shower this time is because my stomach growled when Pan was eating me out.

The water turns cold and I laugh because I didn't know that was possible at a hotel. I guess when you've taken as many showers as I have this morning, it was bound to run out. I hate the cold and shut the water off the moment I shiver.

We have only one dry towel left on the rack. I wrap myself in it and come back out into the main space of my room. I grab a washcloth—the only other option that's not come covered—and dry the wet ends of my hair.

"Pan?" I call out. My room is empty, but that doesn't mean he isn't nearby. I pull open the door that divides our rooms and peek inside. I don't see him, so I call his name again. "Pan?"

The key reader on my door beeps right before it opens.

My skin tingles, feeling his magic before he walks into the room. The man smiles when he sees me and electricity bounces between us. Tattoos peek out from beneath the sleeves of his Nirvana t-shirt and stretch to his knuckles. Jeans cover his lower half and shiny black boots hide his toes. He's got a punk rock meets sex god look going on this morning. If I were wearing panties, they'd be ruined, soaked with need.

"Where'd you go?"

"We missed breakfast, and the little store next to the check-in counter was pretty bare, but I got us some only slightly expired chips, a bag of half-melted chocolate candies, and a Sprite. Not my favorite soda, but it was that or diet." He sets it all on the bed.

"You didn't have to get me anything." I grab the chips and try one. They don't taste stale, so I eat a few more.

Pan twists the top off the Sprite and takes a drink. "You need your energy, Darling." He tries a chocolate, then wrinkles his nose in distaste. "We still have two hours until check out and I'm not done with you."

I laugh. "Please don't tell me you're one of those people who hate —" My stomach rumbles. I cut myself off when a cold sweat covers my skin.

"Darling?"

Bile crawls up my throat. I only get a few seconds' warning before the chips come back up. I grab the little trash can beside the built-in desk and wretch into it.

"You okay?" Pan rubs circles on my back.

I groan and mumble *uh-huh* at the same time. My mouth tastes terrible and my head hurts, but overall I feel fine. "Yeah. That was weird."

Pan reaches for the soda and offers it to me. I feel bad taking it because it's all we have to drink, but we don't have any toothbrushes or toothpaste, and the hotel didn't leave those as complimentary items on the bathroom counter.

"Are you sure?"

"It's all yours, beautiful." He sits on the edge of the bed and watches me with hawk-like intensity. "Are you sure you're okay? Do you want to lie down for a little while?"

"I'm fine," I say semi-convincingly. Now that my stomach is empty, I honestly feel better. Maybe even a little hungry again...for something different. "I think the chips might have gone bad. Once I get some real food in my stomach I should be okay."

Pan eyes me skeptically. He questions if I'm being honest, and I wonder if this weird stomach bug is something I caught from the hospital or the lingering effects of whatever poison Cass gave me. There's no telling what it could have been made from. Neverland has some crazy plants I've never heard of.

Pan grabs what's left of my panties off the floor and picks up the rest of my clothes from the other side of the room.

"What are you doing?"

"Well, we need to get some food in you." He takes all of our dirty towels and tosses them into the bathroom. After doing a quick sweep of my room and collecting the few things I have, he walks through the adjoining door to his room.

"We might as well get on the road, too," he says loudly. I hear a zipper being pulled. There's some shuffling in his room and then the zipper is pulled again. He comes back into my half of our joined space and hands me a pair of jean shorts. "Put these on."

"Okay," I say slowly.

The dark fabric looks a little big. I check the tag and they're a size up from what I usually wear. I don't say anything. Peter—or Pan, whoever did the shopping—got everything else right so far. These were probably the only pair close to my size and in typical man fashion, he probably just assumed they'd fit. I thank him and slip them on. Shockingly, they fit. I tuck the front of my oversized shirt in and grab my shoes.

"Where do you want to eat?" he asks while I'm getting them on.

I think about it as I tie the laces. What's something I haven't eaten in a while? Something I could never get in Neverland and crave now that I'm back.

"K. Kreme donuts!" Those sound delightful right now. The warm, soft dough, covered in glaze that's sickeningly sweet would be divine. My mouth waters in anticipation, but I don't just want donuts. I want something to go with them. I just can't figure out what it is. Finally, it comes to me. "And Chinese."

Pan's eyebrows push together and he looks at me like I've got two heads. "You mean you want Chinese for breakfast and donuts for dessert?"

"No." I laugh. "Together. I think it would taste amazing together."

He hitches my duffle over his shoulder, unconvinced but takes my hand. "Whatever you say, Darling."

⸻

I don't get K. Kreme donuts.

The closest shop was forty-five minutes away. Too far for my rumbling stomach. I settled on the sugar-coated donuts the Chinese Buffet served instead. It isn't what I want per se, but it does the trick.

Pan refuses to try my bourbon tofu lo mein and donuts. Whatever. More for me, and man, do I eat.

My food pooch is so big that I have to unbutton my shorts once we got back in the car, but the bloating is worth every bite.

Since leaving the restaurant two hours ago, all Pan and I have done is sit in traffic. It's horrible. We're stuck, practically crawling on the highway doing fifteen miles per hour. At this rate, it's going to take us years to get to the Florida-Georgia line.

"I got you something." Pan reaches into the backseat and pulls out a brown paper bag.

Inside is a book I've seen but haven't read yet. I know the author, though. She writes about billionaire jerks and the badass babes who tame them.

"This novel is about a guy who fucks things up with his mate. Like royally fucks up. Way worse than Peter and I have."

I arch my eyebrows at him and flip the book over to read the blurb. "I highly doubt that. Whatever this guy, Vic, did to Millie is going to be forgiven because it's fiction. Their storyline is written that way."

"So is ours. We're written in the stars, Darling. Our fates sealed before you were born."

"You're such a nerd." I playfully punch him in the shoulder and then open up to the first page.

Pan chuckles. He grabs my hand and links our fingers together, holding it while he holds the car's shifter. "Just wait. One day, you'll stop fighting fate, and when that day comes, you'll have Neverland shaking in its boots."

CHAPTER 13
Wednesday

I must have fallen asleep at some point because the sun has set and Pan has parked in front of my parents' house. How he knows where they live is beyond me, but I don't think to ask. He knows a lot about my past. It's not shocking that my address is one of those things.

My heart is racing so fast it's hard to focus on anything but my childhood home. Mom and Dad painted while I was gone, changing the exterior from shades of sand to gray and black and re-tiling the roof to match. It almost looks like a different house, but our mailbox is still the same messed-up birdhouse I made in the third grade. I was so excited to have cut the wood during STEM class and build something. I didn't care that the birds hated it.

Until I did.

They never came. Not one. They wouldn't even fly near it. Dad must have noticed how much it hurt because he converted it into a mailbox a few weeks later. He cut a door for the front and added vinyl lettering. Horrible lettering that I hand cut because I thought using a machine or buying pre-cut letters was lame. Our last name, Roberts, was barely legible, but Mom and Dad kept it that way anyway.

My lips twitch at the memory of how mad Mom was when Dad anchored it in front of the house. She wanted something bold and chunky so they'd stop getting their neighbor's mail, and Dad gave her a handcrafted box with artistic flair. The *O* is missing, but Mom kept it just the same. If she hadn't, I'm not sure I'd have the courage to be here.

"Do you want me to go with you?"

I shake my head. This is something I need to do by myself.

I'm nervous.

I know everyone will be happy to have me home, but I can't begin to imagine the pain I've caused. It turns my stomach to try. "No. This is going to be awkward enough. Showing up with my boyfriend will make things worse."

Pan's smile reaches his eyes and it's one of the brightest I've seen either he or Peter do. It makes me warm and fuzzy inside and a little horny. If I wasn't semi-freaking out about seeing my family, I'd probably do something stupid like give him head in front of their house.

"Boyfriend?"

"Don't make a big deal out of it." I grab the door handle to get out, but Pan stops me.

"Wait." He summons his shadow magic. It seeps out of his pores like a dark mist and gathers in his palm. I watch, mesmerized. I don't think I've seen him use magic before, not like this. He takes my hand and some of the darkness slips inside me. Its cold touch twists under my skin and wraps around my arm. Dark pigment tattoos my wrist until it looks like someone has drawn a charm bracelet on me with a single pendant.

A marigold flower.

He kisses my knuckles and the darkness he wields dissipates around him. The bracelet he conjured stays on my skin, it's touch cold but not uncomfortable. "Now I will always be with you. All you have to do is call for me and I will find you."

"Why does this sound like you're leaving?" I think I might die if Pan abandons me today. I need him, not right at this moment, but in my life. My heart races and I begin to panic. I guess deep down, I knew he'd have to go back to Neverland; I just thought I had more time.

I'm not ready.

I don't want to say goodbye.

"Darling." Pan reaches up and touches my cheek. I lean into his hand and let a tear fall. I don't care about hiding them anymore. It's energy wasted since they seem to come whenever they choose. He wipes the droplet away with his thumb. "I am leaving, but not today. I will be out here the whole time, just in case you need me, waiting for the chance to be the hero of your story."

He tilts his head, signaling that it's time.

I spend the whole walk—all three minutes—trying to convince myself that turning around and running back to Pan's car is a bad idea. I owe it to my parents to let them know I'm alive and unharmed, but seeing them again is probably the scariest thing I've ever done.

I raise my fist and knock on the door and my pulse vibrates through my body with each passing second. Maybe this was a bad idea. They're going to have questions I can't answer without lying.

I suck at lying.

I forget half of what I say, get tangled up in the details, and ruin the whole thing. The few times I tried lying back in high school blew up in my face. It was better just to tell the truth.

I take a step backward, ready to retreat, when the front door opens.

Kenny's laugh carries over his shoulder. He's still looking at whoever is inside and hasn't turned to see who's on his doorstep, but his laughter cuts off when he sees me.

My ex barely looks like himself anymore. He's got a beard now, full and red, hanging past his chin. He's thicker around the middle, but I guess that's what comfort does. The thought warms my heart because it means he's happy. My sister is (hopefully) happy too. Despite what we've been through, that's all I've ever wanted for her.

"Hi," I say, my voice just above a whisper.

The color drains from his face as if it's just now sinking in that I'm standing on the porch. Maybe he thought I was a ghost, or maybe that my coming home was a crazy dream. Whatever the case, he doesn't let me in.

Time ticks awkwardly by. Seconds turn into a minute and he's still just standing there. The hand at his side shakes. His other grips the edge of the door so tightly his knuckles are white.

"You're cooling the whole freakin' neighborhood, Kenny." Tyle's voice carries across the house and out to us. She sounds tired and a little frustrated. One hundred percent my sister when she wasn't putting on a show to be the most popular girl in town.

"What's gotten into—" She freezes like Kenny did for a half second and then lets out a scream that steals the air from her lungs.

Tyle pulls me into her chest and hugs me, her big belly pressing against my stomach. "I knew it," she whispers. "No one believed me, but I knew you were alive. I could feel it in my bones that you were okay."

Tyle hasn't hugged me since before college, back when we used to pose for pictures and pretend we were best friends. Our relationship was a relationshit most days, but it was important to our parents that we got along. So, for their sake, we tried when family was around. I hug her back, unable to stop myself from crying again.

"You're so big!" I say through a laugh, looking down at her giant belly.

Tyle laughs, too. She touches her bump and looks down at it with pride. "I've got three weeks left on this little guy."

She sniffles as a tear falls down her cheek. She tries to wipe it away before I notice, but I see it and damn if it doesn't make me feel good. My sister missed me. Pride swells in my chest, then twists into something terrifying. I glance at Kenny, who stares at us, open-mouthed, and look at the tiny details of his face. At the little creases around his eyes. At the size of his belly, round from beer and comfort. He's bigger than any man should be after three weeks of being married. And it's impossible for Tyle to be this far along. *How long was I gone?*

"His sister is in the living room sleeping," she adds.

Sister? I struggle to keep myself from hyperventilating. I look over my shoulder for Pan's car, but it's nowhere to be seen. My hand instinctively goes to my wrist and brushes over my new tattoo. The skin where he marked me is colder than the rest of my wrist and for some reason, I find that comforting.

A calm wave washes over me. Pan said he wouldn't leave. He's just a thought away if I need him.

Tyle links her arm with mine and brings me into the house. It smells like cinnamon and homemade biscuits. Mom used to make the best cinnamon twists for us after school. My heart soars at the thought of her somewhere inside, continuing the tradition for Tyle's daughter after all these years.

"Kenny!" She raises her eyebrows and he seems to snap out of the trance he was in. "Close the door."

"Right." He peers out at the street, then shuts the door and locks it. "Sorry."

"Come into the kitchen." Tyle wipes her eyes and guides me through my childhood home.

Mom made some upgrades. Our fireplace has had a facelift, turning from an old brown to a chic white with a new mantel, and the wallpaper that used to line the space behind the couch is gone. She replaced our burlap-looking curtains with plantation shutters and added a new throw rug over the wood floors. All of these updates were needed, but because I wasn't around when they were done, the place feels less like the home I grew up in and more like a stranger's house.

Tyle opens the door to one of the downstairs bedrooms and puts her finger over her lips to tell me to be quiet. A tiny human sleeps in a crib, her thumb in her mouth, dark brown hair widely spread over the pillow-less mattress.

"This is Wanda," Tyle whispers. "Your niece."

I creep closer to the crib and touch the railing as I look over. She's beautiful, a near-perfect clone of her mother when she was little. "How old is she?"

"Almost three."

Three?

Tyle waves me on so we can let the girl sleep. She leaves the door cracked as we exit and wordlessly walks down the hall to the kitchen. My stomach churns inside itself again. I was gone for three years, maybe longer, depending on how quickly they got pregnant. I feel like I'm going to be sick.

I sit on a stool near the kitchen island in the center of the room. Tyle busies herself, pouring glasses of tea and fetching pretzels from the pantry and a bowl of guacamole from the fridge. I grab a pretzel in hopes that it'll settle the angry sea in my stomach. I dip it in the guac, but the smell makes me throw up in my mouth. I wrap that one in a napkin and eat a plain pretzel instead.

"Oh! I started at a new doctor's office, too," she adds, filling me in on the details of her life I missed out on. "Well, it's not new per se. Just new to me. Since I'm so far along and going to be out on maternity leave, they put me on the telehealth calls. I really like them. The other doctors hate when they have those shifts, so I might see if I can do that full-time and work from home after Weston is born."

"Where's Mom and Dad?" I blurt. I love my sister and have semi-enjoyed hearing about how much has happened in the last few years, but the anticipation of seeing my parents is eating me alive.

Tyle bites her lip. She looks beside me, to Kenny, and then lets out a heavy breath. "They died, Wednesday. About a month after you went missing."

That knot of anticipation I've been wrestling with falls to my feet. The room tilts on its side and spins. Tyle tries to tell me about the accident, but I can't make my mind move past the fact that they're gone. They died, worrying and wondering if I was okay. What's worse, they were on their way to meet another rescue team to look for me. It was my fault. If I had come back sooner, or fought harder to make it toward the surface after going overboard, or hadn't been so hellbent on making Tyle jealous at her bachelorette party, they'd still be here.

A heavy silence fills the room and the air has shifts to darker tones. I feel it linger between us. Tyle takes the nearly empty pitcher of tea off the counter and dumps what's left in the sink. She grabs some new tea bags from a cabinet above the stove and busies herself with the task of making a new batch. I mindlessly nibble on pretzels and simply force myself to do something besides think about Mom and Dad.

"Where the fuck have you been, Wednesday?" Kenny growls, asking the question I've feared most.

A pretzel lodges itself in my throat. I cough and reach for my glass of tea. Tyle won't look at me. She stares at her hands, watching her fingers twist the hem of her shirt. I can see she wants the answer, but is scared of what I might say.

"That's not an easy question." I laugh nervously and feel terrible as soon as the sound leaves my lips.

"Yes, it is." He grips the back of my stool and turns the bench seat to make me face him. "The Coast Guard searched for you for three days, but they found nothing. No trace of your body. Not a stitch of your clothing. Nothing to indicate you were ever on that boat. Tyle felt responsible because she didn't realize you were missing until they disembarked. Everyone, and I mean everyone, was a mess."

The little vein beside his eye bulges. He's angry, but I get the feeling there's more. Things he's been bottling up that have been waiting to come out and I'm the catalyst.

"You can't just show up on our doorstep like it never happened with a bullshit excuse that the answer is complicated. We need answers!" He exhales a breath, his voice growing louder. "I need answers!"

Wanda cries from the other room. Tyle scowls, her head shaking in disappointment. She looks at me, pleading with her eyes for me to stay. "I'll be right back."

Kenny doesn't acknowledge that she's left the room. He boxes me in, one hand on the back of my chair, the other on the counter, and glares at me, waiting for an answer.

My heart races and I blurt, "I don't know where I was, okay!"

Not exactly a lie. If someone were to give me a map, I wouldn't be able to show them where Neverland is. I couldn't tell them how I got there or how I got home. All I can do is give him tiny truths because no one would believe me if I gave them anything else.

"I was drugged and on some remote Island. I didn't know how long I was there until Tyle showed me Wanda. That's when I realized it's been years. Years of my life were stolen in a place where I never saw the sun or the moon, just glimpses of a twilight sky. I had no phone, no television. Hell, I barely had running water, and when I did, it was never hot. I ate things I've never heard of before, hoping they weren't drugged, turned out some of it was—and prayed nothing happened to me while I was unconscious."

"Wednesday..." he stutters. "I...I'm..."

"Want to know how I got back? I woke up three days ago at a hospital in Fort Lauderdale, brought in by a guy who said he found me passed out in a bar. Is that what you wanted to hear, Kenny? Do you feel better?"

Kenny stands upright, giving me back my personal space, but it's too late. Every emotion I felt when I left home comes to the surface. Every fight, every struggle, every betrayal sits on my chest. I slam my cup on the counter and excuse myself. I run to the downstairs bathroom, silently thanking the stars that Tyle didn't remodel it into something crazy, like a wine cellar, and shut myself inside.

My breaths come in erratic spurts. I can't make them steady or make myself stop shaking. Tears run down my cheeks like a faucet left wide open and I hate how much I've cried since coming home. Everything I said was true, but I wasn't prepared for how much the truth would hurt.

I thought Cass was my friend. I let him have a piece of me that I can never get back. It bonded us, even though he knew we didn't have a future. It was obvious to everyone that I had eyes for Peter, but Cass made it seem like he didn't care. He made me feel like I was special when really, he was using me even more than I was using him. I was his twisted ticket home, and he was going to cash it in, even if it meant killing me.

Someone knocks on the door. I wipe my eyes, not wanting to face anyone, but knowing it's inevitable. I don't know who I expected to see. I think I hoped Tyle was lying and that Mom would be there with open arms to pull me into a hug. And maybe I thought it might be my sister ready to tell me that her husband was a dick and that it didn't matter where I was, she was just happy to have me home.

I don't get either of them. Kenny steps into the small space as soon as the door is open, forcing me back a bit. He closes us in the bathroom together. I tense, ready to defend myself if I have to, then relax. I'm not in Neverland anymore. I can trust the people in this house.

No one here wants to hurt me.

"Wednesday." He reaches for my arm.

I flinch back, unsure of why. Kenny has never laid an ill hand on me. The pain he caused was purely emotional, but I can't control the fear. Cass damaged me. He fucked with my mind and I hadn't realized it until this moment. "Stay back." The words automatically come from my mouth.

Kenny looks at me, pale-faced. He steps back and holds his hands up, but it's too late. The bathroom door kicks open, little splinters of wood flying through the air. I jump, startled by the sound but feel Pan's presence before I see him.

Kenny turns around, fuming at the dark-haired devil that broke into his home. "Who the fuck are you?"

Pan takes one look at my tear-stained face and shoves my ex to the side. My sister's husband grabs onto the sink as he falls and somehow dislodges it from the wall. Water sprays out of the pipes. It covers the walls and falls down onto us like a midday rain.

"Come here, Darling."

I don't hesitate and throw myself into Pan's arms. I can't describe the relief I feel having him hold me but the pain of explaining what I went through and reliving each memory in my mind eases to a dull throb. Now, I'm exhausted and, thankfully, out of tears.

Pan, somehow able to read me, senses my fatigue. He lifts me into his arms and cradles me against his chest. He smells like Peter, like cedar and spice, but with modern-day soap too. And if I close my eyes, I can still find traces of Neverland—woods and magic. "Do you want to stay, Darling?"

I rest my cheek on his shoulder. He understands that I'm ready. I thought I could handle coming home, and maybe if Mom and Dad were here it would have been different, but I can't stay. It hurts too much. I need to grieve their deaths without judgmental eyes watching me, or pitying me. I can't do that here. "Take me home, Shadow."

Kenny begins to stir on the floor. Pan sees it at the same time I do and we seem to have the same thought. It's time to go.

Pan carries me even though I can walk, and I don't fight him on it. I feel safe in his arms. Nothing can touch me so long as we're together. I chastise myself because less than twenty-four hours ago, I didn't trust Pan. Now, he's the only person in this world that I do.

Tyle steps out of Wanda's room, her eyes wide with fear when she sees me being carried out of her house. "Wednesday?"

Pan walks past her, ignoring my freaked-out sister, and takes us out the door. Kenny runs after me. He tries to grab Pan by the arm, but he doesn't know he's picking a fight with a creature from another world. He doesn't stand a chance.

Pan turns and swings on instinct, effortlessly carrying me with one arm and fighting my ex. Tyle screams from the doorway when his fist collides with Kenny's face. Wanda cries in her arms. Everything is falling apart and I'm helpless to do anything but let it happen.

"Put her down," Kenny demands, rushing Pan again.

Pan throws another punch and his fist hits Kenny square in the jaw. My brother-in-law falls to the ground, nose bloodied, lip busted, and this time, he stays there.

"I know you," Tyle says, her voice hardening. She steps off the front porch more certain the longer she stares. "You're him. The guy from the boat." She sets Wanda on the floor, ignoring her cries, and runs after Pan. She beats her fists against his back and claws at his shirt as he carries me to the car.

"No!" she screams. "You're not taking her again. You're not taking the only family I have left."

Guilt gnaws at my insides, but I'm paralyzed both physically and emotionally. I hide my face, ashamed that I'm not standing up to my demons and telling Pan to let me stay, but the truth is I don't want to.

I don't want to look my sister in the eye and see the resentment.

I don't want to walk around my parents' house, haunted by their ghosts.

I don't want to see Kenny live out his happy-ever-after while mine is postponed due to circumstances that stretch beyond this world.

All I want to do is leave.

Leave my sister.

Leave my childhood home.

And go back to Neverland.

CHAPTER 14
Wednesday

I stare out the window as we drive away.

The world moves past us in a blur of colors, but I don't care enough to look at where we're going. I just want to leave.

My heart cracks open with each mile we drive and the guilt swallows me whole. My parents are dead. They never got to meet Wanda and will never see their newest grandchild, Weston. They'll never meet Peter or Pan. I won't get to walk down the aisle with my father or have one last dance with him. I don't even know if he was there for Tyle on her big day.

Our car stops moving and I focus my gaze on the landscape in front of me, actually making the effort to see where we are. An acre of bright green grass decorated with thousands of marble and slate headstones awaits. My heart pounds in my chest and a cold sweat breaks out across my skin. Pan opens my door and a vice squeezes my chest. I can't take a deep breath. I try and try and each bit of air my lungs grasp is smaller and smaller.

"Darling." Pan grabs my arms. "Easy, love, you're getting yourself worked up."

I can't hear what he says. The sound of my heartbeat in my ears drowns everything else out. The light around him starbursts. I'm shaking and hyperventilating and...*oh my god, my parents are dead*!

"Darling?" Pan cups my cheeks. I look up at him, but all I see are silhouettes cast in shadow. He feels so far away and the tunnel to make my way to him is narrowing. I think I might puke or pass out or...

Pan kisses me and everything goes quiet.

I close my eyes and let him take me away from the darkness, let the layers of the world pull back until all that's left is him. Pan's lips pull me out of my mind and back to him, where nothing matters but us.

"Found you," he whispers, pulling away. I look into his eyes and almost cry when I see one is blue. I have both Peter and Pan, the two halves of my soul together again. Even though it only lasts a moment, that one second feels like home.

The blue iris is swallowed by darkness and I'm left with Pan. The strange shadow man I wanted to hate, but somehow ended up falling for. I'd laugh if I weren't on the verge of crying again. If I were planning to stay in this realm, I think therapy might be good for me. I've fallen too hard, too fast, for men I have no business being with too many times.

"Are you all right, Darling?"

My gaze drifts past my dark-haired savior to the entrance of the cemetery. I assume this is where my parents are. How Pan knows is beyond me, but I don't want to ask. I'd rather assume his magic led us here than go down the darker paths my mind strays toward.

"You need to see them. It'll help."

I shake my head. I can't go there, not if I want to hold on to the paper-thin shred of strength I have left. Seeing their names in the granite would be the straw that breaks me. "Take me away from here, Shadow."

Pan sits on his heels, the name I've only used a few times, cutting deep. I feel his sorrow as deeply as I feel my own. I look down at the tattooed bracelet on my wrist and finally understand its purpose. It's not just a mark to remind me of him, it links us, broadcasting my emotions and possibly even my thoughts. Pan felt my fear in the bathroom at Tyle's house, which is why he barged in to save me.

He didn't know what was wrong. All he knew was I needed him.

And he came.

"Where should we go, Darling?"

"Neverland. I don't want to be here anymore."

"Shh, you don't mean that."

"I do! I can't have my only family be Tyle!" The car closes in on me again and it feels smaller and smaller the longer I sit. Pan instinctively takes my hand and helps me out of it. He pulls me into his arms and a fresh wave of overwhelming sadness has me burying my face in his chest. "You don't know what it's like to have a sister like her."

He threads his fingers through my hair, running them from my scalp to the ends, trying to soothe me. "I know that she has never fought for you before today. Her attempt was pathetic, but it was something."

He uses his magic to draw my eyes upwards. I hate that he's seen so many tears running down my face in such a short amount of time. I've never been this person, someone who cries at the slightest of things and emotionally spirals out of control. Tyle was dramatic enough for the both of us and I always thought she was stupid for feeling so deeply. I understand now that she couldn't help herself. These feelings are literally exploding out of me. I don't want to be this pathetic, emotional disaster, but I can't make the tears stop. They're just there, doing their thing, as steadily and consistently as my beating heart.

"Give her a chance. You're all she has now, too."

"She has Kenny," I mumble bitterly.

Pan chuckles, the sound light as air, and kisses my forehead. He shifts my body to be under his arms and we start walking. I bristle until we go in a different direction, toward the sidewalk and not the gravestones.

He takes me to an ice cream store two blocks away. The bell over the door rings when we step inside. A woman comes out from around the corner and greets us with a smile. "Afternoon. What can I get you lovely folks?"

I scan the menu. Everything looks delicious and it hits me that it's been years since I had ice cream, not weeks. I've been dairy-sensitive since I was a kid. It tears up my stomach if I have too much, but a little here and there never hurt too bad. I chew on my lip and weigh my options. There's so much I want, but destroying a public bathroom or, worse, the small one of a hotel room would be mortifying. "Can I get your dairy-free vanilla in a small cup?"

"Sure." She lifts the glass door, encasing all the flavors up, and scoops a large sphere of ice cream into a paper cup. "Do you want to mix anything in it?"

"I can do that?" There only used to be one ice cream store, a chain-type place, that did customized mix-ins. I perk up and look at my topping options. "I want to add cookie dough pieces and caramel drizzle."

The woman makes my ice cream and hands it over. I take a bite and it's like an orgasm in my mouth. I forgot how amazing ice cream tasted. I can't even tell it's dairy-free.

"And for you, sir?"

"Vanilla."

"Do you want to add any toppings?"

"Nope." Pan looks at me and winks. "It's my favorite flavor."

I choke on a lump of cookie dough. My gaze jumps to Pan's eyes, hoping to get a glimpse of deep blue again. There's not even a speck within the shades of gray and black, but there is a lot more brown. He has a ring of gold surrounding the darkness that wasn't there before.

Pan pays for our treat with a credit card and then hands it to me. "Here"

"What's this for?"

"You're going to need money while I'm gone. Spend whatever you need. There's enough to last ten lifetimes."

I spoon a scoop of ice cream into my mouth and shake my head. "I don't want it."

He tucks the card into my back pocket and grins. "Who says you have a choice?"

I roll my eyes. Yesterday, I would have been angry with him for trying to control the situation. Today, I feel no ill will through the bond. Every threat, even those made with the straightest of faces, was playful. I don't think Pan knows how to tease, but I can tell this is his way of trying.

We walk down the sidewalk and look at displays in the shop windows. We don't buy anything, but it's fun to look at anyway. Eventually, we reach the end of the little plaza and head back toward the car. I toss my empty ice cream cup in a nearby trash and let the silence fill the gaps between us. Pan doesn't seem to notice, but my mind is racing. The closer we get to the cemetery, the heavier this weight feels.

"I mean what I said, I want to go back." I steal a glance at Pan from the corner of my eye. He doesn't look at me. I'm glad. I don't think I could tell him what I'm going through if he did. "I don't feel right being here. My skin aches and my chest feels hollow. The only time I don't feel out of place is when I'm with you and you're leaving."

Pan sighs, letting out a heavy breath. "I can't bring you back, Darling, not until it's safe."

I bite my bottom lip, struggling with what to do. Peter blatantly asked me if I knew who was behind my poisonings and I didn't say anything. I'm scared Pan will be angry with me for keeping a secret. His brows furrow and I realize I'm sending some big emotions through our bond. He waits patiently for me to explain the fear and nervousness. I take another minute, trying to build my confidence, and say, "What if I could help?"

"The only way you could help is if you know who wants you dead." He laughs humorously, as if that notion is impossible, but as the silence thickens again, his smile falls. He knows I'm hiding something. I can feel his curiosity. "Is there something you're not telling me?"

"Yes..."

"Wednesday!"

"I'm sorry, but I haven't decided if I could live with his blood on my hands."

"He tried to kill you. Twice!" Pan runs his fingers through his hair and stares up at the sky. He's angry, so terribly angry, but trying to calm himself so he doesn't blow up at me.

"He had a good reason," I say sheepishly. Trying to justify what Cass did to me is like trying to explain the logic of a revenge murderer. I may sympathize with what brought him to that place of desperation, but it doesn't absolve his actions. Cass needs to be taught a lesson. I just don't want that lesson to cost him his life.

"Being Belle's huntsman isn't a good enough reason."

Wait, who? "Belle? Like Tinkerbelle?"

Pan nods. "Tinkerbelle is the single worst thing to happen to Neverland. She is behind ninety percent of my problems."

"And the other ten percent?" The *thump, thump, thump* of my heart tells me I already know the answer. It's me. I'm the second-largest problem in his life. Always fretting if I'm safe. Always wondering if our relationship's damage runs deeper than our lust can heal. In the silence that stretches between us, I meet his gaze and his truths are all over his face.

The worry.

The regret.

The love.

"I'll let you know once you tell me who hurt you. It will save a lot of time and unnecessary pain if you'd just tell me which pirate she has under her thumb."

It never occurred to me that Peter would venture into the Cove to hunt for my attacker. It should have because he won't look at the Lost. They're his friends. His family. He'll never see the betrayal coming. "It was Cass."

"That motherfucker." Pan turns to a nearby tree and slams his fist into it. The trunk splits down the center from the base of its branches all the way to the roots, allowing warm light to spill through the newfound opening. He curses under his breath about balancing nature, then holds his hands to the broken bark. His dark magic surrounds the tree to heal it. It only takes seconds to fix what he broke, but once the shadows thin and return to him, Pan looks miserable, almost as bad as Peter did in the hospital and he sways on his feet.

I reach out to steady him, scared he's going to fall out. "Are you okay?"

"Don't touch me!" Pan jumps back before I can comfort him.

My heart shatters because I don't understand what I did wrong. Sure, I kept a secret for a few hours, but does that justify the surge of anger and him retreating like this? I feel as if Pan has cut me deeper than Peter ever did. A strangled sound leaves my throat as I try to breathe and hold back my pain.

Pan sees me struggling and curses under his breath. "Damn it, Darling. I'm sorry," he says with a sigh. "It's not you. This is all me. If you touch me I could hurt you and that's the last thing I want to do."

"How? You touch me all the time."

"I'm what the Fae call a Reaper. It's my job to keep the balance between life and death. Right now, I'm emotional and weak from healing the tree. I don't know if I can control myself and touching you isn't worth the risk."

I chose to focus on the life part of what he says, not the death. I can't think about how many people he may have killed being a Reaper or how many lives he probably took in the hospital when he mentioned feasting on the souls the doctors could bring him. I don't want to think of him as something dark or evil. So, I choose not to. "You keep the Island alive."

"And as many souls on it as I can. There, my power is endless, but here...every breath I take fights my purpose. To survive here with you I have to take years from others' lives. Years they'll never know are missing, but are gone nonetheless."

"And you do that by touch."

He nods. "A bump here. The brush of a hand there. Little by little, I keep myself alive, conscious of what I'm taking because I never let myself get weak enough to lose control."

"Peter didn't..."

Pan shakes his head. "He wouldn't let me feed our body. When he blacked out, I walked through the hospital searching for those who were in the most pain, the people who were ready to move on but whose families wouldn't let go and took what was left of their lives until I was strong enough to control the hunger. The thing that made me..." Pan looks out at the gravestones. "That monster is death himself. A creature created for the sole purpose of ending lives."

I look at him incredulously. "Are you saying the god of death, Hades, made you?"

"I'm saying that the thing that made me, as well as many others, can be found throughout your history. Their names change with each culture, but their purpose remains true. The Grim Reaper, Hades, Osiris, and Odin were all of Fae descent. Each of them was a reaper who fed off the living to have immortality."

"So, something came and took my parents from me? Something like you?" I'm angry again. If there is a monster living in this town, stealing the lives of innocent people just to prolong its own, I want it dead. I want to hunt it down and kill it myself for taking away the people I love.

"Your parent's accident was tragic, but a Reaper did not cause it. What a Reaper did was come and ease their suffering. They created a calmness in their minds and helped them pass into the next life."

"And stole the years they should have had left."

"Yes."

"I think I'm going to be sick."

"Would you rather they suffered? Slipped into a coma, kept alive by machines for years while stuck in the between, waiting for a death that might not come?"

I think about my time lost in the between. It was cold and empty of any signs of life. There was no way to tell time or determine how many days were lost. It was an endless prison where I was stuck in my mind, reliving every moment, both good and bad, over and over again until I regained consciousness. "No. I guess not."

"Our job isn't easy, but we are helping people. Not hurting them."

I feel a little better knowing someone was there to take their pain away, but the sting of their passing is still fresh. It's hard to separate my anger for the creature that stole their final breath from Pan. They are the same species. The same type of monster. "So, you've never stolen years from someone who wasn't dying?"

Pan lets the silence hang between us as he walks to the car and leans against the hood. "No."

Well, that wasn't very clear. I need to know if the man whose dick was inside me this morning is a good person or not. I moved past the murderous aspect of our relationship because it was only my life, but if he's taken others...others who had many healthy years left with no natural cause for it to be shortened...I don't think I could let that go "No you haven't or no you have?"

Anger simmers in the tether that binds us. I don't think it's directed toward me. I don't know how I know; an instinctual feeling, I guess. Whoever it is toward, it's lethal. "No, I have."

"What the fuck?" I yell! I can't believe it. He's a killer. A cold-blooded killer. "Pan!"

"No!" He's up and in my face with a swiftness only Neverland's magic can create. Darkness clouds his aura, seeping from his skin in a thin mist. Pan is so close his breath heats my cheeks, but he doesn't touch me. "Do you remember Mr. Banefield?"

"The man who used to live across the street from us? He died of a heart attack." I rear back, shocked. I always thought it was weird a thirty-four-year-old man could die that young. When we went to the funeral his family was as surprised, too. They said he was in perfect health, never even had a cavity. "Was that you?"

"Yes."

Gods damn it. Of course, it was. He literally told me he'd been a shadow in my life since I was a kid. He needs human life to exist. I just don't understand, "Why him?"

"Because he was obsessed with you!" Pan roars. "That man had pictures of you and your sister in his room. Hundreds of them. He would watch you play and...” Pan growls deep in his throat, his eyes darkening even more than I thought possible. “He was a bad man with bad intentions. I killed him because he wanted to hurt you, just like I killed others I found who were like him."

Fucking hell, Pan.

If that's true, how can I hate you for saving me? Can I really crucify you for helping to rid the world of pedophiles and creeps? I guess with him life isn’t just black and white. It’s shades of gray and everything in between.

"I don’t care if you hate me. Your world is a better place without that twisted fuck. Now, if you’ll excuse me, I need to feed." He tosses me the keys from his pocket. I catch them, barely, and stare at the ring.

Panic festers under my skin. I can't drive a stick shift. I need him for so much more than just to drive a car, but, frankly, I really do need him for that. "Where are you going?"

"I don’t know." He tucks his hands into his pockets and heads back to the plaza we'd just left.

"Where am I supposed to go?" I call after him. I hope he can feel the desperation I'm drowning in through our bond. He can't abandon me, not here. Take me to a hotel or someplace safe, then let me go.

Don't.

Just.

Leave.

Pan stops walking, his shoulders slumping forward. He feels it. I know he does, but it's not enough to bring him back. "Doesn’t matter. As long as your heart is beating, I’ll find you. Perks of being soulmates, Darling. It might take a while, but we’ll end up together one way or another."

I pace the floor of my newly rented hotel room. My thumbnail is chewed down to nearly nothing. Every time I stick it in my mouth and search for more to bite, my finger stings, aching in protest, but I can't help it.

I'm stressing, freaking the fuck out, because Pan has no idea where I am.

I got the closest hotel within walking distance to his car—that I may have left parked in the cemetery—but I'm still worried we're too far away from each other. I don't know how this shadow bond works or how strong our tether is. Can he feel my worry if he's down the street? Across town? On the other side of the world?

How about in a different realm?

I open the door, hoping to see him walking down the hallway to me, but there's no one out there. The ugly green carpet doesn't even have a discarded dinner tray. It's completely empty. My anxiety creeps higher and higher. My hands already won't stop shaking, and it's only been a few hours.

How am I supposed to survive when he leaves me behind?

I don't know why I'm so worked up. Pan's disappearance should be at the bottom of the list of things my brain can be hyper-focusing on. If I was to be thinking of him at all, it should be how he's out there robbing people of precious years.

I wonder if they can feel when he takes from them. Do they become tired and fall asleep? Do they get a headache and take medicine to alleviate the ache? Or is the process painless to where the affected don't even notice?

I flip the security lock so the door stays propped open, close it as much as the lock allows, and then fall onto the bed. I try to think about something else, anything else, but my mind is restless. After staring at the ceiling for ten minutes, I give up and take a shower to pass the time.

Standing under the water, and letting it fall over my head and down my face, I can almost imagine I'm back in my bathroom at the treehouse. It makes it easier to pretend I'm in Neverland again like this, waiting for Peter to come home after a long day of searching for newly resurrected magical creatures. I hated how he would leave me alone for hours, but I loved when he would come back to me.

"Thinking of me?"

Fear has my fist shooting out on instinct. The moment my hand collides with skin, my brain recognizes Pan's voice. It hits me again how much Cass has fucked with my mind. I hadn't realized how traumatized I was until Kenny tried to touch me. Mix my near assault on Pan into the equation, and it's safe to say I've got some shit to work through.

"Oh, my god, Pan. I'm so sorry."

"Relax, Darling. Didn't even hurt." He tilts his chin upwards to show me the nonexistent red mark from my attack. His skin is flawless. Absolutely perfect.

I punch him in the shoulder—on purpose this time—and cross my arms. "Where have you been? I was worried about you."

"I had some business to take care of."

"You mean lives to steal." I shut the water off and shiver. I hate the cold. My body isn't built for it. My nipples pucker and I love how Pan's gaze darts down to my chest, though I'll never tell him. I grab a towel and begin drying myself, starting with the girls. "Do you feel better now? Less murderous."

"I feel something." Pan rips the towel from me and throws it on the floor. My hands shoot above my head all on their own and press against the wall. My feet spread a little more than hip-width apart. He smirks approvingly. "Want to find out what that is?"

Pan knows what my answer will be. He drops to his knees, hands settling on my hips, and dips between my legs. "You have no idea how hard it was not to touch you when you were in Neverland. The fact that you couldn't be mine made me crave you even more than I already do. But to feel your worry through our bond." He kisses the inside of my thigh. "Your desire. It's more than I can bear."

Pan finds my center and sucks my folds into his mouth. His tongue is fire against my skin and I melt into the warmth. He eats me, feverishly working to bring me to my knees while magically keeping me upright. I try to fight against the sensation. For some reason, my body's response is to pull away. The fact that I can't intensifies everything.

"I'm still mad at you," I say through heavy breaths. Pan kisses the inside of my thigh again. He presses two fingers inside me, and if it weren't for his magical bond holding me upright, I'd be a puddle on the floor.

"I'm sorry," he says, his voice dropping to a husky growl. "Forgive me?"

I forgave him the moment he walked through the door. I think the ease I felt earlier had nothing to do with my shower and everything to do with our souls finding each other again. The world could fall to pieces around Pan, and I'd feel safe and completely satiated with life because he creates a level of comfort inside me that's incomparable. My only complaint would be that I haven't had enough time to enjoy him—a fixable problem with an easy solution.

"Yes," I pant, riding the rush of my climax. I'm putty in this man's hands and he knows it. Hell, he could probably blink in my direction and my panties would be wet.

Pan peppers kisses along my side up to the swell of my breasts. He then sucks my nipple in his mouth, playing with it, licking it while teasing the other one between his fingers.

"Shadow." I thread my fingers through his hair and pull his mouth off my chest. I need to feel him. His hands aren't enough and his mouth only leaves me hungry. I physically ache inside and there is only one way to alleviate the pain.

Pan's smile is feral, his thoughts not far from mine. "Tell me what you want, Darling," he says, looking into my eyes. His black irises are more honey brown than any other color, and I can't figure out why, but at this moment, I can't bring myself to care. I don't feel bad craving Shadow anymore because Peter is within him somewhere. When I have one, I will always have the other.

My Peter Pan.

"I want you," I tell him truthfully. "Always." I kiss him, just enough to leave him hungry. I want him to feel the same desire I'm drowning in, and not because it's traveling through our bond. "And forever." Another chaste kiss.

Pan grabs my thighs and lifts me, a deep growl vibrating low in his throat. My legs wrap around him and the spell on my limbs breaks. My hands can't find his body fast enough. I touch every inch of him, committing the hard edges of his body to memory because I know this is our goodbye. Something in him is changing. I can see it just as much as I can feel it. I know he can't stay.

But I don't want him to go.

Pan unbuckles his belt with one hand while effortlessly holding me against the tiles with the other. His pants fall to his feet and I don't hesitate to make him mine or ask for a condom. I'm ready. I want to feel every inch of him without a barrier between us.

Pan grants my wish, lowering me onto him and pushing inside me in such a way he's both forceful and tender all at once. The way he moves, the way his lips hunger for my body, this is more than fucking. He's claiming me and I'm not ashamed to admit that I am his.

Forever his.

And he is mine.

Pan grips the back of my neck and uses gravity to drive himself deeper. I cry out his name, *Pan, Pan, Pan* as my back grinds into the wall, filled with more pleasure than should be inhumanly possible.

"God, Wednesday," he says. I kiss his shoulders, his neck, anything I can reach. My moans of pleasure echo in the small space and I almost don't hear him when he whispers, "I love you." He kisses my neck and I shiver, possibly from the words more than the touch. "I love you so much it hurts."

My body comes alive with tingles at his admission and I come again. Pan finishes inside me shortly after my release. He holds my body against his chest, probably coming down from our mingled waves of emotions. I fold around him until he grows tired of holding me and sets me on my feet.

"I mean it." Pan tugs his shirt off and reaches to restart the water. "I do. I love you and not because you're my soulmate, or Wendy's reincarnation, or because Peter wants me to. I love you because of who you are." He pulls me into his chest and looks down into my eyes. "I love your beautiful soul. Your willingness to forgive. Your patience. I love you for your ability to simply be you."

"Thank you." I don't want to say it back, not like this, in some dingy hotel shower post sex.

I know it's silly, but I always hoped for some grand gesture like you see in the movies. Kenny is the only other man to say those words to me and the first time they left his lips he was drunk. He didn't remember saying them the next day, or maybe he did and regretted it. When he finally coherently said those three little words, the romanticism of the experience was lost.

Pan takes a step back, realizing I'm not going to return the sentiment, and washes himself. He hands me a towel once we're done cleaning up and I hate the tension builds between us as the night carries on. Even as we lay in bed, pretending to be a normal couple and watching a movie, I can hear the *tick tick tick* of time slipping away.

Pan glances out the window, a frown tugging at his lips, then tries to focus on the television again, but he's a man divided.

"What's wrong?"

"I don't know." Pan sighs and walks to the window. He draws the curtains and stares up at the night sky. "But something isn't right in Neverland. It's calling to me."

"You should go."

Pan looks over his shoulder at me, his face a mix of emotions. "You're right, I should. Doesn't mean I want to, though." He grabs my hand and draws me into him, kissing me so tenderly and with such love that I don't know how to respond. My heart breaks because this truly is our kiss goodbye.

Tears well in my eyes when we break away. "I need you to know why I didn't say it back."

Pan's gaze softens when he looks at me. I wish the love I see eased the pain of goodbye but, if anything, it makes the sting worse because I know leaving is just as hard for him as it is for me.

Maybe even harder.

"You don't need to say anything. I know what's in your heart." He runs his thumb over my dark tattoo. "Remember?"

I nod and swallow the lump in my throat. "Okay. Good, but you need to know I won't say it until you come back. I'm holding those words in my heart so you don't forget me."

"Darling." He holds me in his arms. "I could never forget you." I relish in his warmth and the way his magic wraps around me like a blanket. The cold feels like dewdrops on a spring day. Beautiful. A little annoying. But magical.

"Will you see me off?"

I shake my head and nuzzle into his chest. "That's probably a bad idea. When it comes to the moment you actually fly away, I can't promise I won't beg and plead for you to stay."

"I would. In a heartbeat."

"I know, and I can't ask that from you. The Lost might be in danger. They might need you." I step out of his arms and sit on the bed, my back to the door. I know that if I watch him go, I'll follow. The chord that links us together will pull tight and I won't be able to stop myself from trying to make him stay. "Go. At the very least, you have Cass to deal with."

Pans face hardens. "Yes. Him." He glances out the window again. His jaw ticks with frustration at whatever is pulling him away. He's silent, fighting a war within himself.

"If I don't go now..." He lets the sentence trail off. I understand what he's not saying.

I stand again and kiss him on the cheek. Pan reaches for me, to pull me into him once more, but I dodge the embrace. It's time to cut the cord and let him go. Besides, it's only for a few days. I can survive a few days on my own. I lived for years without him in my life. This won't be easy, but it will be doable.

I walk to the bathroom and shut myself in it. I slide down the door and bury my face in my hands. I don't need to look into the room to know the moment Pan leaves. I feel his departure as an anxiety attack wraps itself around me. My heart thuds in my chest as my soul fights to chase after its other half.

This ache is unlike any pain I've ever felt. It runs deeper than the hurt from losing my parents or the bite of betrayal love has repeatedly given me. The pain twists itself around my spine, seeping venom into my blood until the world is nothing but shades of gray.

Something inside my chest snaps and the pain is as real as if my bones were breaking. I scramble to the mirror and lift my shirt. Every movement, every breath is excruciating. I don't see any marks in my chest or back. There is no sign of physical damage to my body.

But it hurts. So. Bad.

I open the bathroom door and make my way to the bed. The room has the beautiful scent of earth, sage, and morning dew. The perfect mixture of both Peter and Pan. I lay on the mattress and hug Pan's pillow to my chest and my finger brushes against the tattoo he left me with.

I wonder where in the night sky he is and if he's crossed into Neverland yet. I hope he can't feel how much it hurts to be left behind, even though I know it had to be done. I don't know how far our bond stretches, but I hope he's out of reach.

I don't want him to know what it feels like to have a broken heart.

CHAPTER 16
Pan

Leaving Wednesday is the hardest thing I've ever done.

My darkness fights to stay with her. It pulls, kicks, and claws at the threads of her realm. It pleads with my body, doing everything in its power to return to my other half. I wonder if this is what it felt like for Peter when his soul split from his body and became me.

Agony.

I soar through the sky, fighting the urge to turn back with every star I pass. The only thing that keeps me going is knowing I'll be back for her in a day. Two tops.

Cass is no match for me. His powers are weak from lying dormant all these years. All I have to do is find his ass and he'll be dust in the wind, and then I can bring our Darling back.

My heart hangs heavy when the bridge between Neverland and Wednesday's world comes into view. The moment I cross into Neverland, I'll never feel her again. Her lips will belong to my other half and I'll be in the backseat watching them live out their lives together, forced to feel their emotions secondhand, like a reader and their favorite book.

It will be torture.

But I'd rather be an active bystander in their lives than nothing at all.

"Get ready, old friend," I say to Peter as the veil between our world and hers draws nearer.

I hesitate for a moment to take the last breath I'll breathe. Once I cross over, I won't just be losing the chance to be with Wednesday, I won't be human anymore. I'll never smell the crisp scent of ocean air or taste the cold sweetness of ice cream. I'll never feel the fullness of air in my lungs or the warmth of another hand in mine.

The temptation to abandon Neverland and be selfish is almost as strong as my desire to stay with Wednesday. I could easily do it, live out the rest of her life in Peter's body, saving souls from suffering.

A scream breaks through the barrier between our worlds. I react, the pull to save whoever is in need jarring me out of my selfish indulgences. I soar through the bridge, prepared to be sent back into darkness and kicked out of this body, but I stay in control.

"Peter?" I think to him. I flex the fingers on his hands, waiting for him to take over, but his resistance doesn't come.

My mind is my own. Empty. Void of any traces of my other half.

"Peter!" I demand as I soar above the clouds.

He's quiet and that makes me worry. He should have regained control. I've never lived in his body for this long after crossing over. I draw my magic inside myself and search for a sign of life, but there's nothing. Peter is gone.

A cannonball shoots up at me from a ship below. The force of air whooshing by me throws me off balance. I tumble in the air, narrowly missing a flock of seagulls. I find my footing after a handful of somersaults and soar higher into the thicker tufts of cloud.

"Come down, little brother. We need to have a chat!" James yells from below.

I call to the sea, wanting to make waves for the old codfish. I would love to see his boat topple over and for him to be drenched like the rat he is. I hate the man. I would have killed him off years ago, but he's the only being on this island that Peter has shown attachment to.

I don't know why.

All James has done is aid Belle in destroying Neverland. He's hunted souls for her to feed on, growing her powers in the process. He is the singular reason why that bitch is alive, and she's the reason Peter's Wendy died.

"Peter!" James yells. The boom of another cannon sounds and a ball whooshes past me on the right.

I clear my throat and test a few words, trying to muster a dialect that resembles my other half. "You expect me to play nice when you're trying to kill me, brother? That's bad form if I say so myself."

He shoots another round and misses by a mile. If I didn't know the man, I'd say he was missing me on purpose. "Where's the girl, Peter?"

I fly down and land on his ship. "If you kill me, you'll never know," I taunt. Even if he leaves me alive, I'll never tell him. I'd rather die than aid in that crazy bitch's plan to rule Neverland. She'll suck the Island's magic dry and turn our home into a wasteland.

"I don't want to kill you," James says beneath his breath.

I see the conflict on his face. It's puzzling because I've never noticed it before. He blindly follows Belle's orders, but today he's at war with himself. *Odd.*

"You'd have been dead long ago if that were the case." He laughs humorously, but his shoulders fall forward. The man looks tired, a feeling I've never personally experienced until this weekend with Wednesday. I sympathize—another new emotion for me—and sit on the forecastle railing. James climbs the steps from the deck to be beside me. "I have no choice but to try, brother."

"That Fae bitch's claws run deep?"

"You have no idea." He turns his head and I can see bite marks along his neck. Reapers steal time, but the rest of the Fae steal lives. They need the blood of the living to stay young. A few drops will satisfy their thirst, but most are wicked and kill for the fun of it, spilling enough to live for years, tasting as many souls as possible.

"She's safe."

"She'll never be safe," he says solemnly.

I don't waste my breath arguing. Belle will never have our Darling. I'll die before even a drop of her blood is spilled.

James's shoulders slump forward. He's a defeated man. Broken. Trapped in a meaningless existence. I growl, not liking these new revelations. In my eyes, James has always been an enemy, but to Peter, his brother is kin to a victim. I don't like it. Makes it harder to want to see him dead.

The smells of ash and cedar tickle my nose. I search the horizon for the origin. Neverland burns as large plumes of smoke rise into the air. How did I miss that when I flew in? More importantly, why can't I feel the Island crying out to me?

"She'll burn the Island to ash looking for her." James pulls a sword from his sheath and hands it to me.

I have no need for weapons. The Island and my magic have always been more than enough, but a strange tickling sensation in the back of my mind urges me to take it. I do, without a word of thanks, and shoot up into the sky. I fly toward the treehouses and to the souls I've kept hidden all of these years, pleading to the gods I'm not too late.

My home is on fire. Bright red flames lick each house that Peter built. My hands may not have physically twisted each branch and mudded each wall, but I feel ownership of it.

Our reservoir that holds the dirty water from our bathrooms is dry. I reach for the clouds, calling to the sky to put the fire out, but it doesn't respond. Like the ocean that ignored my calls to rock James' boat, the Island isn't listening.

I groan, frustrated, because I don't know how to stop the flames from taking over. I grab fistfuls of dirt and throw them on a nearby lick of fire but it does nothing. I snap a few fronds of an unburnt palm and fly to the water. I dunk them and then drop them on a roof, hoping it will make even the slightest of differences, but all it does is create more smoke.

I cough and a memory deep in Peter's mind tickles my consciousness. Smoke inhalation is just as deadly as fire. It hits me that my souls, the Lost, could be trapped inside somewhere, dying.

I fly to the nearest treehouse, not caring about how I now have a body that can burn, and make my way to the porch. Heat sears my flesh, but I fight through the pain and kick in the door. The walls are orange with fire lights. Dark smoke fills the air, trapped inside by a ceiling that hasn't yet collapsed.

"Xyris," I call out while walking from room to room, searching his house for any sign of life. My relief that it's empty is short-lived. The roof falls into in the bedroom. Pieces of the floorboard break away and fall to the ground. His house is collapsing, taking everything he owns with it. I feel sorry for the loss of his treasure, but grateful his life isn't among them.

I use the opening in the roof to fly out of the hut, ignoring the burn of the flames as they lick my arms and legs. I fly to the next house and comb through it as thoroughly as I did the first. I search for my friends and then move on to another once I'm convinced the house is clear. One by one, I double-check that my friends are safe.

The last treehouse is the worst. The fire's flames are so hot they're blue. I shouldn't go in it; Peter's body is already blistering, but I can't shake the guilt already festering about not searching *every* treehouse. I fly around it twice, searching for a way inside that won't lead to my own death. There's a window on the back half engulfed in flames, where the fire is only shades of red.

I raise my arm to protect my face and break through the glass. The air turns to steam in my lungs. I can barely see, let alone breathe, but still manage to call out. "Hello? Is anyone there?"

Smoke surrounds me. I crouch low to the floor. Everything is shadowed or burnt. I can't see shit, but I do my best to make my way through the house. I find Aria huddled on the shower floor. The fire somehow hasn't touched her, but it's close.

"Aria?" I shake her shoulders and tap her cheek, but her eyes won't open.

Something falls in the other room. If I had to guess, I'd say it was either part of the ceiling or the floor. Whatever the case, it's not good.

I lift Aria's unconscious body into my arms and the pressure of her skin against mine has my knees buckling. Peter's body is teetering on the brink of exhaustion. It smells of charred clothes and burnt hair. His pants have caught fire, melted in places, and sticks to his legs. His shirt is a barely there thread, holding on by microfibers. But every bit of pain we suffer is worth it because knowing that our family is safe is all that matters. Aria's death would have been on my conscience if I hadn't searched for her. I couldn't live with that. I don't know why the Island is rejecting me, but it's still my job to keep it and the people we love safe.

I look around at what's left of her treehouse. There's no clear exit, and every second I stand here searching for a way out, the fire grows bigger. Smoke fills my lungs and this body doesn't like it. I cough and cough. Unable to free myself from the dark noose that's wrapped around me. Spots cloud my vision. Peter's body can't take much more, and I can't reach my magic to heal him.

I run toward the nearest wall and leap. I turn my back to it, so I go through the flames first and shield Aria as best as possible. I feel each bite of the fire and the razor-sharp sting of wood as it splinters into me. I feel the air try to lick my wounds and fail to lift us out of danger as we fall onto the ember-covered ground.

I land first, taking the brunt of the fall. The wind is knocked from my lungs and, for a brief moment, I wonder if this is what it feels like to die. The pain of doing something as simple as catching my breath ravages every neuron inside me, but I don't let it take control. I roll onto my side and force my legs to carry us away from the flames. I fall to my knees the moment it's safe and lay Aria on the ground.

I touch her blistered cheeks, terrified that I'm too late. I hate when people die. The curse of the Reaper is to see what their lives should have been. Absorbing their years is to absorb their future. Each life I've taken weighs on me. Their shadow lives haunt my dreams. It's why I chose to stay in Neverland. Here I have the power to ward off death, but I can't give life.

"Aria!" I cry out. She doesn't respond.

I place my ear to her chest and by the grace of the gods and all the stars in the sky, it beats. The sound is quieter than a breeze passing through a meadow, but it's there. I beg my powers to wrap around Aria and heal her body. The dark shadows I carry don't respond. They stretch, just out of reach, to where I can see them but aren't close enough to wield.

I beat my fists against the ground. Frustrated. Pissed that Peter won't return. It's his fault my powers are fading. I'm not meant to exist like this. I rummage through Peter's memories, searching for a sign of what to do, until I find an ancient lesson on CPR.

I watch the scene play out like a movie in my mind. The details are as crisp as if they were played on the television in Wednesday's hotel room. I pinch Aria's nose and breathe clean air into her lungs, then press on her chest, grasping at strands of hope that I can push the smoke out of her body.

I breathe and push, and breathe and push, refusing to accept that I've failed.

Aria gasps. Her eyes fly open and she coughs. I roll her onto her side and pat her back, helping to clear her lungs and the relief I feel can't be described.

Aria sits upright. Her breaths are shallow and labored but her lungs move on their own. She looks at me, eyes wide.

"Peter?" she says and the fear in her voice would have sent me to my knees if I wasn't already on the ground.

Something falls over my face. I'm pushed forward, onto my stomach, and then everything goes dark.

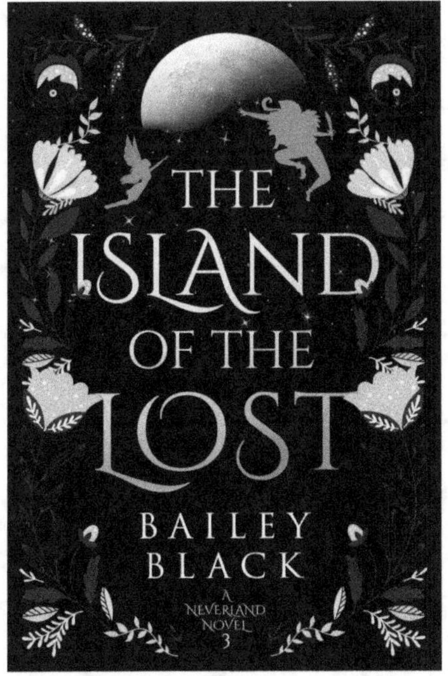

Prologue

I left this world broken hearted.

With wounds held together by bandages and duct tape.

I was dying inside, trying to put the pieces of my life back together. Unsure of up from down. Dreading spending each night alone because the memories of my sister and my ex-boyfriend's betrayal would haunt me.

It's funny how the cuts on my heart that I thought would never heal are barely scars.

How time, as unreliable as it may be, can mend all wounds.

Well, most.

The pain I feel now, runs deeper than anything I've ever felt. I live another life every time I close my eyes. I feel Wendy's love for both Peter and James as if it were my own and it blurs the lines of everything I know. But walking in her footsteps each night is better than existing in this purgatory because there I get to see Peter.

I get to touch him in their stolen moments.

I get to hear his voice whispering to me in the dark.

And I get to feel her guilt for loving one brother more than the other.

Turn the page to finish the adventure.

WEDNESDAY
A CHAPTER FROM ISLAND OF THE LOST

It's been days.

Days of waiting and hoping for Pan to come back to me.

Days of having takeout delivered because I didn't want to miss the moment he returned.

Days that drag on, minutes feeling like hours, and he still hasn't come back to me.

I look at yesterday's pizza box, still sitting on the table with a half-eaten slice inside, a war wages inside of me. On one hand, I should eat something because I skipped breakfast. What little of the plain cheese slice I tried to eat last night is all I've had in the last twelve hours. On the other hand, my nerves are so shot, I've barely been able to keep anything down.

Is it worth it to eat if I know I'm just going to throw it up later?

I roll onto my side and hold Pan's pillow to my chest, wishing it was him. Wendy Darling's emotions have twisted with mine, pushing away the anger and fear I clung to while in Neverland. I shouldn't let her feelings consume me. I would be better off hating both Peter and Pan for turning my life upside down. I *should* be thanking them for bringing me back to the life I begged and plotted to return to.

Instead, I'm drowning in depression, missing a man I never wanted to love, and desperate to return to a world no one believes exists.

I hold the pillow tighter, fully understanding why Wendy Darling donned a pen name and twisted her stories into the beloved fairy tale. She would have been put in an insane asylum had she told her truths any other way.

I've wondered more than once if talking to someone about what I went through might help ease the pain of missing the other half of my soul. At the very least, it would help me sort through how I feel and what I want. I might even figure out how to separate all things Wendy from my everyday existence and only draw on her experiences when I'm ready.

But the only person who knows I'm not dead is my sister, Tyle, and she is the last person I want to see.

Her life is perfect.

I huff out a laugh that is swallowed by a sob. Of course, it is. Tyle got everything I wanted in life, right down to our childhood home, while I'm stuck pining over an impossibility.

I bury my face in what's left of Pan's scent. Thanks to my breath, the cotton smells more like stale pizza than him, but it still has a hint of earth and magic. Soon, though, even that will be gone.

And then I'll have nothing.

A new wave of sadness has me crying again. I've given up trying to control my tears, let alone stop them. Centuries of longing flow through me, and every time I close my eyes, I let in a little more pain. Watching Wendy live her life, feeling it as if I'm experiencing it all myself, is torture. Yet, I willingly put myself through that pain because living in her reality while I dream is better than existing on my own.

A *rap, rap, rapping* on the door has my heart skipping a beat. No one should be knocking. I have the *do not disturb* sign on the door specifically to avoid human contact, and there isn't a soul alive who knows where I am.

Except for my Peter Pan.

Oh my gosh!

I wipe my eyes, excited and hopeful that Pan has returned. Or maybe it's Peter. I don't know who I want to see more. They're the same man, yet different all at once. Pan will likely barge into the room and take me in a hungry kiss. Peter will probably tuck his hands into his pockets and give me that lazy grin of his. Both will have me on my back within minutes of returning, and while I'd rather see them at the same time, having either one would send me over the moon. I love them both separately and equally and would be happy to see either.

But if I had to choose...

Hell, I'm not sure I could.

I run my fingers through my hair and try to make myself look somewhat decent. I should have taken a shower and I'm kicking myself for not thinking to be ready for when the other half of my soul returned, but there's no time now.

I hurry to the sink, put on some deodorant, then brush my teeth for all of thirty seconds. My mouth feels cleaner and minty, and while I'm too gross for sex (I need to shave pretty much every inch of my body), I don't feel like a cavewoman anymore.

He knocks again.

"I'm coming!" I yell. My heart races with each step and my stomach lurches. I'm so excited I could puke, but I try to hold it back. That would ruin our reunion. Although even if I did, we'd probably laugh about it later.

A small arrow of fear strikes my bubble of excitement because three days is just a few hours in Neverland. I doubt Peter has found Cass yet, but if he's here, that means one of two things. Something terrible has happened or it's safe enough for me to return.

I'm praying it's the latter because being in this world again is torture. Time moves too slow, forcing me to feel more than I ever thought possible.

I reach for the chain on the door. My fingers fumble, the connection between them and my brain broken, like a song on a fuzzy radio station. Bits of what I want them to do eventually break through the static and I finally slide the chain, twist the latch on the door, and tug it open.

My heart falls to the floor so hard that I have to bite my tongue until it bleeds to keep my tears at bay.

It's not him.

Of course, it's not.

"Thank God. You're here!" Tyle throws her arms around me and pulls me into a hug. She then cradles my cheeks in her hands, looking at me like she's scared I'll disappear the moment she closes her eyes.

"How did you find me?"

Tyle drops her hands and we awkwardly stand in the hallway until it hits me that she's waiting to be invited in. I step to the side and open the door wider. Her nose wrinkles once she's inside. I sniff the air. It has a mild sour smell, so I don't judge her for the face she makes, even though I know she's judging more than just the room.

"Someone left a note a few days ago stating you were here, in this room, and to come get you." She lifts the pizza lid. A fly scurries out, and I'm glad I decided to skip lunch. "I thought it was a joke. Kenny had told Kierra that you'd come back the other day, she went to a dark place after you died, and I thought the note might have been her way of coping with an old wound. But it was eating at me. So, I came." She pokes her head into the bathroom and relaxes when she realizes it's empty. "Where is Peter?"

"You remember his name?" I ask, surprised. Tyle used to go through boys so quickly that she'd name them all *handsome* so she wouldn't call her new toy by the old toy's name. The fact that Peter's name stuck after knowing him for less than ten minutes is shy of a miracle.

"How could I forget? Peter has haunted me ever since I met him. It took me a minute to match his face when I saw him at the house, but there was no mistaking who he was once I did." She lets the part about him being the man who took me hang in the air. I don't finish the statement for her and desperately hope she doesn't ask.

"He left," I say as impassively as possible. She won't understand that every minute he's gone, I die a little inside. Hell, I don't even fully understand. All I know is that I feel like a ghost in this world without my Peter Pan.

Tyle takes a hard look at me and frowns. "You're sad about that?"

I shrug, not having a good explanation. "It's complicated. You wouldn't understand."

"I understand perfectly, Wednesday. It's called Stockholm syndrome. You were held captive by him for years and you fell in love. It's perfectly normal, but that doesn't make it okay." She reaches out and touches my arm. "I can help you through this."

I jerk free of her touch, horrified. She doesn't know anything. Peter Pan didn't hold me prisoner. He was my friend. He saved me more times than any man should need to. She's wrong! "I don't need help, Tyle. I'm fine."

I turn my back to her, walk back to the bed, fall into the heap of blankets, and grab Pan's pillow again. I close my eyes and wish for sleep, desperate to see Peter's face again.

"This place is a dump, Wens." Tyle tries to shift the conversation, and that tone, the one laced with judgment and disappointment, comes out of hiding.

"Why are you here, Tyle?" I don't look at her. I don't want to see her glowing with love as she grows her baby. Yes, I'm still bitter. Just because I don't love my ex—or want him anymore—doesn't mean I can't still be angry.

Family is supposed to be forever.

They are supposed to be the people you can always count on.

My family isn't in this room. They're back in Neverland because those people are more loyal to me than my own blood.

"I was worried about you." The bed dips as Tyle sits beside me. She pushes the blankets back until I have no choice but to look at her. Dark bags peek through her concealer. She looks tired and years older as her makeup folds into the fine lines of her face. "When that man took you again..." She bites her lip and shakes her head. "I thought I'd lost you."

"Stop." I push up onto one arm and glare at my sister. "Stop pretending that you care about me. You don't. You haven't since the seventh grade when you woke up and decided that we weren't twins anymore."

"Wednesday." Tyle swallows hard and closes her eyes. I give her a minute, although I'm unsure why, and wait for her to compose herself again. "I'm sorry."

"Sorry can't change the past." I get up and start cleaning my mess because I don't know what else to do. I can't just sit here and pretend that singular word erases years of trauma, because it doesn't.

"I know." She sighs, taking the empty bag of chips from my hand and carelessly dropping it to the floor. "But damn it, Wednesday, you're all I have. We have to stick together."

"What about Kenny?" I raise my eyebrows, curious about her response.

"Things with Kenny are complicated. We got married because of Wanda, but we don't love each other. He's been cheating on me since before the wedding." Tyle drops into the chair, unconcerned about crushing my only clothes.

"Sucks, doesn't it?" I cross my arms, wanting to hold on to my anger, but as I watch my sister wither from the strong woman who didn't care about anyone but herself to a broken shell of that person, I can't stay mad.

"You know what they say." She forces a smile and tries to sound playful, but I can hear the tears on the brink of breaking free. "What goes around comes around." She sniffles and then stretches her smile wider. "Enough about me. What are you doing, Wednesday? Why are you in this hellhole? This place reeks, and, no offense, you look like shit."

The look Tyle gives me warms my heart because if Mom could see her, she'd be proud. Tyle has mastered the *I'm disappointed but still love you* face.

I'm not sure what to say. Outside of what I did a few minutes ago, I haven't made any effort to brush my hair, put on makeup, or even find matching clothes since Pan left. All I've done is sit here and cry.

And wait and cry.

And eat and cry.

And then throw up because I'm so upset and anxious and ready for him to come back that I can't keep anything down.

But if Tyle is here because Pan sent her, I can't help but fear he knew that he'd be gone more than a few days. The color drains from my face when it hits me that he may never return. Pan planned for my sister to find me because he knew I wouldn't leave this room. Ten life-times of money sits in his account and I would have spent half of it wasting the years away.

Just. Waiting.

The shred of hope I have that he'll return shatters. I bury my face in his pillow again, overwhelmed with a new round of tears. Tyle shifts and holds me in her arms. She can't begin to understand my pain, and still, she keeps me in her embrace, trying to ease the ache.

"Wednesday." Her voice cracks as she fights her own wave of emotion. "Come home."

"I don't have a home."

"Yes, you do. Your home is with Kenny and Wanda and me. We've missed you." She pulls back and looks me in the eyes. "We love you."

I lean against the side of the bed and curl my knees into my chest, wrapping my arms around them. I don't know if I can be in that house without Mom. It hurts too much.

Tyle sits beside me and touches my back. "It doesn't have to be forever," she adds, reading my mind. "Just until we get you settled, sort out the whole death certificate thing, and get a job. You're welcome to stay as long as you want, but I know you won't."

I laugh humorously at the thought of living with my sister and her husband. The three of us under the same roof, playing house, sounds like a nightmare.

"How have you been paying for this?" Tyle asks, looking around the room again.

"Peter left me some money." I pause, tempted to keep everything Peter and Pan related to myself, but I need help moving and probably selling the car. So, I add, "And a car."

"He gave you a car?" she asks, eyebrows arched.

I nod and laugh when I say, "I don't know how to drive it. It's a stick."

"Oh, honey, once you learn how to work a stick, it comes naturally," my sister says with too much enthusiasm, trying to cheer me up. She wiggles her eyebrows and I can't help but laugh with her. It feels so good not to be in constant competition with each other.

Neverland years aside, I can't remember the last time we sat together and got along without pretending.

"Please, Wednesday, even if it's just for a few days, you need to get out of this place. It smells like puke in here." She wrinkles her nose again.

That's because I can't keep anything down.

I let my head fall against the mattress and stare at the popcorn ceiling. As much as I don't want to be around Kenny or in that house, I don't want to be alone. Heartbreak is harder when you're alone. "I don't know."

"Okay. No pressure, we can talk about where you'll live later." She holds up her hands in mock surrender. "What about lunch then?"

"Huh?"

"Lunch. Let me take you to the mall. We'll go shopping and get something to eat. My treat."

I'm about to tell her no when my stomach cramps. I touch my belly, feeling its angry rumbles. I'm still not used to all the additives this world puts into its food. I throw up half of what I eat, which is why I've mostly had chips the last two days. Something about the grease and the salt mixes with me. It's the only thing I can keep down but I probably should put something besides crap in my stomach. And I really do need some more clothes.

"Fine," I concede. "Let me take a shower and get ready."

"Oh, thank God."

"What?"

"I didn't want to say anything, but you smell terrible." She grins, teasing and telling the truth all at once.

I grab a pillow that isn't Pan's and chuck it at Tyle as I pass the bed. I don't forget the years of bullshit she's put me through, or how I still hate her, but a small part of me is glad Tyle showed up.

With her here, I'm not alone.

PAN

A CHAPTER FROM ISLAND OF THE LOST

Someone kicks me in the side, causing a sharp pain to ripple through my body. The ache lingers, refusing to fade away, despite the Island's usual reach to mend the broken.

Seconds pass and my magic doesn't heal me. It should have. Just like it should have called to the sky for rain and the ocean for waves. Yet, its power eludes me. I can feel the pulsating energy as it stirs beneath the earth, vibrating with an almost taunting presence. I can taste the metallicness in the air, but I can't make any of it listen to my pleas.

A voice slices through the silence, etching itself like a scar in my mind. "I thought the great Peter Panning would be more difficult to capture." I recognize it without needing to see the face to know whom it belongs to. Belle—Cass and Emmit's sister—kicks me in the side again and says, "Pity."

The rough burlap sack over my head is abruptly ripped away, revealing a dimly lit room. My eyes take a moment to adjust to the pale glow of fireflies in lanterns, but I recognize where I am as. I'm in a holding room deep within one of the caverns beneath the stone castle carved into the mountainside. One of the many forgotten dungeons the Fae King used to keep.

Peter's friends, the Lost—Aria, Heidi, Emmit, and Xyris—hang in iron shackles from their wrists alongside me, their unconscious forms swaying slightly. The only one awake is Emmit. His head moves in the slightest, warning me. I don't know what the warning is for, but whatever it is, I'm not supposed to do it.

"Tell me, Peter." Belle's voice echoes in the barren space while her footsteps click ominously. She remains hidden in the dark, her presence felt rather than seen. "Are we going to do this the easy way or the hard way? I do so hope you make things difficult. I haven't had any fun in ages."

Belle finally steps into the dim light wearing a glittering green floor-length gown. The woman looks ready for a ball, not a torture session, but that is Belle. Her vanity is her greatest weakness, aside from her hunger.

I force a grin and try my hardest to sound like my other half. It's been so long since Peter has seen Belle. I doubt she'll notice the difference between my eyes and his, but she'll recognize my voice. I sound too much like James.

I was cursed with the parts of Peter that he didn't want, including anything that tied him to his old life. Like his accent. And most of his memories. "Good to see you, Belle. You don't look a day over two hundred."

Belle studies me. I've only had a voice for a few days. Trying to hide my natural accent is difficult but not impossible. *But do I sound like Peter?*

Her lack of response makes me nervous. I blow Belle a kiss and her nose wrinkles. She looks at me like I'm a dog who just shit on her shoes and then dragged all of my crap on the train of her dress. She schools her face to seem impassive, but I can see the rage pooling beneath the surface. Good. That's something I can work with.

"Where's the girl?" Belle demands, her tone laced with impatience. I feel a small sense of relief, but I don't let it linger. I'm on a ticking time bomb, the fuse growing shorter the longer we're in each other's presence. My only hope is that Belle's lack of patience will make her careless.

"You have a room full of pretty girls. Which one would you prefer?" I reply, feigning innocence. There is only one woman worthy of Belle's time, The Darling, and she will never have her.

With a swift motion, Belle's open hand lands a stinging slap across my face. "Please play games with me, Peter," she says, fury bleeding into her sarcasm. "I want so badly to make you bleed."

I press my lips together and swallow a knot of nervousness. My heart ticks faster. The moment she tastes my blood, she'll know I'm not Peter. She will drain me, mercilessly, for the mere pleasure of it and absorb what's left of my magic into her veins.

But that's not the worst part. When a Fae drinks the blood of another, they gain access to their memories, though it's the last drop that holds a person's greatest secret. Belle would bleed me dry for that drop alone because it would lead her to Wednesday.

I can't let that happen.

"Do it, Belle. I dare you," I challenge, my voice trembling slightly. "Cut my skin. Taste my flesh because without my shadow it will be ash in your mouth. It will take back every year you've stolen and you'll be nothing but dust in the wind."

"Liar!" she screams. She grips my chin between her fingers and tries to compel me into telling the truth, but she's weak. Her magic wraps around my words, but they aren't strong enough to rip them from my lips.

I bite down on my tongue until I taste iron, then lick my lips, purposely staining them red. I pray she doesn't call my bluff, but this is something Peter would do. "Want to find out?"

Belle huffs in frustration and shoves my forehead. My skull cracks against the stone. Pain—a feeling I'm not used to and have only felt secondhand—wraps around my head and shoots down my spine. It's intense and dizzying, but I laugh because that's what Peter would do, too. He'd poke the bear over and over until she lost her temper. Before the Darling arrived, everything was a game to him.

One he always had to win.

"Your blood may be no good to me, but I have a buffet of souls to choose from. Where should I start, Peter?" Belle walks past our friends, dragging her nails across each one's cheek, spilling blood as she makes a turn around the room. "Which pathetic little half-mortal do you love most?"

"Leave them alone, Tinkerbell!" Emmit roars. He pulls against the iron cuff. The metal sizzles as it sears another layer of his skin away. I know it hurts, it has to, but Emmit hides the pain behind a mask of indifference. "They aren't a part of this."

"Sweet baby brother," she coos, her words laced with false affection as she turns her attention to him. "Don't you understand? I'm doing all this for us."

"Liar!" he growls. "You've only ever thought about yourself. This has nothing to do with me."

"Do you know what our father had planned for you? He was going to ship you off to war. He wanted you dead." She touches her chest, giving an Emmy-worthy show of practiced care that he sees straight through. "I saved you."

"You killed him. You killed everyone."

"I did it for you," Belle claims. Her voice cracks and I might've believed her if I didn't know better. But I do know better. Just like I know about the souls she bleeds to feed her thirst and how the more vital the memory, the stronger her magic is. I know that her borrowed power lasts days, sometimes less, before it wanes and she's forced to feed again.

"You killed them to be queen. You don't care about me. You never have," Emmit counters, a vicious smirk curling his lips. "Too bad the Island saw through your bullshit and picked someone else to rule."

Belle smacks him and her nail slashes across his cheek, leaving a deep gash that seeps crimson. "Now look what you've made me do," she mutters, a mixture of irritation and disappointment clouding her face. Belle heaves a sigh and strides over to Heidi, unchaining her and dragging her by the wrist toward Emmit. "Drink," she commands. "Once you taste the power their memories hold, you'll be so much stronger."

"No."

Belle cuts Heidi's wrist with her thumbnail. Blood wells up and leaks down her pale skin. "Your body won't heal itself without help anymore. Drink!"

"No!"

"Why not?" Belle demands.

"Because she's my friend," Emmit says defiantly. "I won't do it. I won't be like you."

"Put her life to use or waste it. I don't care. Either way, she dies,"

Belle coldly retorts. She slides her thumbnail across Heidi's neck, slitting the artery that feeds the brain, then drops the body. Blood leaks out of our friend at an inhuman speed, a puddle of deep red stains the dirt and seeps into her clothes.

"Stop this, Belle! Stop her bleeding," Emmit pleads, desperation creeping into his voice. He pulls at the cuffs again. They've rubbed his skin raw, down to the muscle. If he doesn't stop, they'll eat through his hand.

Belle pretends to consider for a moment, feigning kindness. She shakes her shoulders and a shower of golden dust fills the air. She catches a handful of it and tosses it at Emmit. He stops writhing, his body frozen in place, save for the movement of his eyes.

"I think I'd rather have you watch her die," she remarks, a sinister edge to her voice. "All you had to do was take one little taste. You could have healed her the moment your strength returned, but you chose to let her rot. What happens next is on you."

She steps forward and cups his cheeks in her hands, ducking down to meet him at eye level. "I am not your enemy, little brother. One day, you'll see that."

Belle's attention shifts back to me. "As for you," she declares. She walks to each of the Lost and tosses her golden dust on them, ensuring that time cannot touch their motionless forms. "Every day you delay, another one of your friends will die." She stands before me, her gaze locking with mine.

I clench my teeth, refusing to break eye contact. We've found ourselves in another game, one I'd happily lose to kick her in the stomach if I weren't pretending to be someone else.

Now would be a good time to come back, Peter. My thoughts are torn between chastising him for abandoning us and all the ways I'm going to kill this bitch when I get free.

"I will drain every last drop of their blood. I will extract their souls, and I will obliterate any chance of them having a life beyond this one," Belle threatens, a wicked smile playing on her lips. "I've been generous by allowing you to keep your pets." She pauses and smirks. "Did you think I didn't know? I know everything, Peter. I've kept my word to your brother all these years, but the Darling changes everything."

"What did my brother promise you?"

"You have... seven friends, correct?" Belle's voice drips with malice. "Will you let them all die? Or perhaps just this one? The choice, Peter, is yours."

"Belle!" I shout, my voice filled with a mixture of desperation and defiance. "What deal did James make?"

She chuckles wickedly and turns the corner, leaving me alone with nothing but my thoughts.

Read Island of the Lost

**Fall In love with a
Bailey Black Book Here**

BOOK 1 IN THE BROKEN LOVE SERIES

Piper

Most people don't think about the day they'll die. They coast through life, blissfully unaware of how their time is ticking away. I wasn't like most people. I welcomed death, wanted her to take me away from the prison I called life, but she refused. I tried twice only to survive. And then, when I thought I had nothing left it came.A reason to live.Rex was a small, unexpected ray of light my world of darkness that blossomed into a beam of sunshine. I thought, maybe this was why Death didn't take me. Maybe she knew that if I held on a little longer things would turn around. But the third time Death came to my door wasn't by choice. Someone else brought her, and I fear this time she might take me.

Rex

Being the son of a country star sucks. My parents are never around, I move every year or so, and I have no real friends. Everyone around me has an agenda. Everyone except Piper Lovelace. I can't get that girl to notice me. Trust me I've tried.Thankfully, fate stepped in and gave me the break I needed. I've got her attention, now I need her to give me a chance.

**Fall In love with a
Bailey Black Book Here**

Enemies to Lovers, High School Bully, Athlete Antihero, First Love, Girl Next Door, Completed Duet

BOOK 2 IN THE BROKEN LOVE SERIES

She's beautiful. Fierce. Nothing at all like the girl I used to know, which is absolutely terrifying because Danika Winters is the only person outside of that room who knows the truth. She could ruin me, and I'm not talking about my reputation. I couldn't give two shits about what the kids at St. A's think. I'm talking major, life-altering, jail time ruined. I'll do whatever it takes to keep her quiet. Even if it means destroying the only person I've ever cared about.

Asher Anderson is a dick.

We aren't friends, so when he seeks me out in the cafeteria on the worst day of my life, I'm suspicious. When he tells Liam Heiter that we're dating, which couldn't be farther from the truth, I want to kill him...Until I see Liam's reaction.

Liam—my best friend, the guy who crushed every hope of us *officially* being together—is jealous. He has never looked at me this way and I love it.

So, I play along. Maybe watching me with someone else will make Liam suffer like I have the past four years. And maybe, just maybe, he'll come to his senses and realize we belong together. It's not like I actually *like* Asher. At best, I tolerate him. What's the worst that can happen?

Small town, Opposites attract, Cowboy, New girl in town, Unexpected parenthood (+denial)

Josh

Josh Andrews hadn't expected to meet the girl of his dreams in a church parking lot—especially not while his best friend was hooking up in his truck. But there she was, parked two spaces away, pretending not to notice his predicament. Layla was gorgeous, sharp-witted, and completely immune to his charm.

He should have walked away. Instead, he couldn't stop thinking about her. Layla wasn't like the girls who usually fell for his easy smile and smooth lines. She challenged him, saw right through him—and he liked it. For the first time, he wanted more than just a fleeting connection. He wanted her.

Winning her over won't be easy, but Josh has never backed down from a challenge. And Layla? She might just be the one risk worth taking.

**Fall In love with a
Bailey Black Book Here**

Second chance, The dare/bet, Insta chemistry, Learning to love, Shared
Pasts

I've sworn off men forever! Okay, not forever, but for a few months.
After my last hook-up, my vag needs a reset because the last man to
touch me broke it in the worst of ways. Not a problem until my new
dance partner comes into the picture. He's turning into my forbidden
fruit, tempting me in ways I didn't know possible.

I have three months of celibacy ahead of me and eight weeks to
whip my new dance partner into shape.

Someone save me.

SCAN TO READ A
SAMPLE

Fake dating, Second chance, Friends to lovers, Everybody can see it, Short and Spicy novella

A wedding. A lie. And regret.

I'm in over my head with not one but two ex-boyfriends at the same wedding. Both of which I haven't seen in over a year. When the one who ripped my heart into pieces backs me into a corner, I grab the other and kiss him.

Yup. This is how I ended up fake dating Noah Ruckers, and let me tell you, it's an emotional roller coaster. I thought I'd put my feelings for him behind me. We spent years as friends after our break up, nothing more. But no matter how hard I try I can't forget what his lips feel like. Or the way his arms wrap around me.

In two days, I'm walking away. There is no future for us. But that doesn't mean I can't pretend.

**Fall In love with a
Bailey Black Book Here**

Fake dating, Second chance, Friends to lovers, Everybody can see it, Short and Spicy novella

Holly Flynn is a leprechaun who grants wishes—but with a dangerous twist. Each wish comes at a price: once it's fulfilled, the "victim" forgets everything before their wish—and her.

When a gorgeous stranger asks for one unforgettable night, things take an unexpected twist. The chemistry between them is electric, and soon, Holly's struck by a terrifying thought: She doesn't want him to forget her.

Then, a week later, he knocks on her door. And he remembers everything.

Why does he remember, when no one else does? Is it fate—or is her magic betraying her?

**Fall In love with a
Bailey Black Book Here**

How About a Fantasy Adventure?

Dive into the completed Neverland Novels. Characters have been aged up for this darker, grittier version. If you like your fairytale retellings with hot, ruthless, morally gray love interests, you'll enjoy this series. The Lost Darling is the first book in the main storyline. Please read this series in order.

Twisted Fairy Tale, Peter Pan Retelling, Multiple Love Interests, Morally Gray Males, She's Mine, Scorching hot lost boys, Spice, and more!

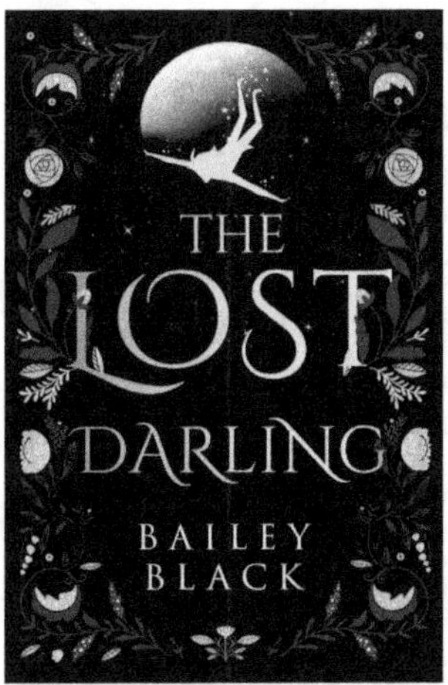

Second star to the left and continue until morning.

I got that line tattooed on my wrist the day I turned twenty-one. So much symbolism in such a simple sentence. At the time, it was a nod to the future and the infinite possibilities to come, while reminding me to remember the past and to look for magic in the world.

Growing up, nothing was ever what it seemed. The shift of leaves on a tree was a faery skipping by. Shooting stars were a chance to make wishes. Shadows were souls stuck between this world and the next, mirroring a life they once had.

My imagination was limitless, the world a wonderful adventure waiting to unfold.

It's easy to lose that sense of wonder with the weight of life on your shoulders and I wanted a reminder to get me through the hard days.

Most importantly, it was an ode to the boy who earned the title of my first crush, even if he was animated. Peter Pan wasn't a *save the damsel* kind of prince. He was daring, and selfless, and took care of the ones he loved. He was a friend to all but never afraid to fight the Pirates when their moral compass broke. Wendy was an idiot for leaving him. She rushed home to a heartless world full of men willing to lie through their teeth to get down her pants.

But that's the beauty of a book, the characters are perfectly flawed. Damaged just enough that we still love them. Whereas reality is nothing but empty promises and baggage the size of mountains.

The day I got my tattoo, I would have given anything to be whisked away into a fairytale. My world was crumbling, and all I wanted was to go back to when life was simpler. I didn't realize I had sealed my fate in ink.

Branded myself as one of the Lost.

Neverland was everything the stories made it out to be. Beautiful. Full of magic. Filled with handsome men and debonair pirates. But the author of my favorite tale left out one crucial detail.

In order to get there, you have to die.

A witch in a world where magic is illegal, A revenge mission, A rescue mission, Death. People die. Sorry, not sorry, 2 love interests (not a RH and not a triangle), A touch of enemies to lovers. He falls first she falls harder

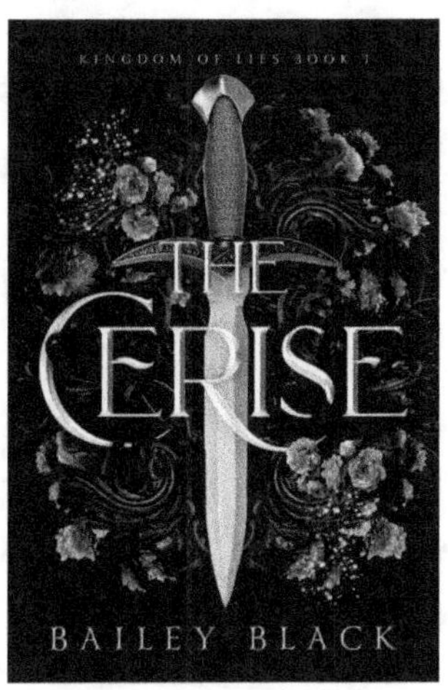

I had a plan. Find the soldier who killed my family and make him pay. It should have been an easy feat. I'd done it over a dozen times, taking out each member of that regiment one by one, but the mission went sideways. It all started with the man in the woods. The one my webs of magic couldn't sense even when he stood before me. Then my partner made a mistake, and now he's lying in one of the Crown's dungeons, fighting for his life. I couldn't leave him to die, but I couldn't just walk into the castle either.

Or maybe I could.

With the help of some unexpected allies, I entered the Culling—a one-in-a-lifetime chance to become queen. I have no interest in winning the prince's heart, or the crown. My only goal is to get into the castle, find my friend, and get out before someone realizes I'm a Cerise.

But when the welcome ball turns from a grand event into a nightmarish dance of death, all eyes are on me. As if that's not bad enough, the soldier, the one who took my family, he's here.

If you loved "The Selection" by Kiera Cass and "From Blood and Ash"
by Jennifer L. Armentrout, get ready to fall in love with this
enchanting fantasy romance!

130

**Fall In love with a
Bailey Black Book Here**

ABOUT BAILEY

I've always wanted to be a writer. I remember my first time really trying to write. It was after I saw Practical Magic and I knew there was more to those characters. Being the creative ten-year-old I was, I managed to write a solid two paragraphs on my mother's dinosaur of a laptop. Fast forward fifteen years, when I was a new stay-at-home mom with no time for friends, let alone a life. I rediscovered my love for reading, which turned into a love of writing. There were A LOT of bad stories in the beginning (those aren't published) but I eventually honed my craft and grew brave enough to publish them in the world.

I'm not a full-time author as of yet. I'm still a mom and a wife and somehow balancing a job along with all the responsibilities tied to adulthood. My writing hours are slim, but man when I dive into a world it's hard to get me out of it.

So far, I've been lucky enough to have readers just as enamored with my characters as I am. It still humbles me that there are readers and bloggers out there willing to take a chance on my stories. So while this is a little bit about me, it's also about you because without your support I wouldn't have a career.

Thank you, from the bottom of my heart, for always believing
on me.